Murder in AsiaTown

By Dan Hanson

Cover image
Head of the Lion from the Kwan Family Lion Dance Team
at the Cleveland Asian Festival.

This book is a work of fiction. Names, characters, places and incidents are either a products of the author's imagination, embellished or are used fictitiously. Any resemblance to actual events, locales or persons, living or dead, is entirely coincidental except where permission has been granted.

Dan Hanson, Publisher
868 Montford Rd.
Cleveland Heights, OH 44121
www.danhansonbooks.com

Library of Congress Control Number: 2024922292

ISBN 9798343668032

Dedication

To James Francis "Bud" Sweeney,
wife Helen and kids Patricia,
James Francis Jr. and Terry.

Acknowledgements

Thanks to Margaret Wong, Johnny Wu, Lisa Wong, George Kwan, Debbie Hanson, "Uncle Jim" Sweeney, Oanh Loi-Powell, Henry Fong and all the restaurants and businesses of Cleveland's Chinatown and AsiaTown.

Chapter 1 – The Present

Ren Wu was tired. He had been pouring over old newspapers, documents and anything else he could get his hands on for his company's latest project, a history of Cleveland's Chinatown and AsiaTown.

His eyes burned but he was resolved to finish another month of stories from ancient editions of old Cleveland newspapers. Usually the work would have been divided with his two partners but since he was the only one of the three fluent in both Mandarin and Cantonese, the tedious task fell on him.

His partners Dick "DJ" Jamieson and Peggy Powell were working on other aspects of the project. The three colleagues had seen their fledgling company take off after working on a photo and video documentary of the Cleveland Cultural Gardens. Their help in solving several murders in the Cultural Gardens led to a lot of attention for their small firm and helped land them this account.

Ren's right hand scrolled through image after image. Unfortunately for him, the decades old newspapers were saved as picture files, not as searchable text, so he had to painstakingly read each headline and decide if it was what he was looking for.

"Just a few more," he thought as his eyelids grew even heavier. Scroll. Scroll. Scroll.

Wait! What was that? His eyes opened wide and he scrolled back to a previous image. The headline read "Chinatown Killer Caught." But what really woke him up was the picture of the killer.

He was looking at a grainy black and white picture of himself.

Chapter 2 – The Present

Ren Wu couldn't wait to show his colleagues what he had found. They were supposed to meet for dinner at Siam Café on East 40th and St. Clair at 6 PM. It used to be a Red Barn fast-food restaurant and you could still see the shape of the barn from the front.

Normally, anticipation of a dinner of Pad Thai would dominate Ren's thoughts on the drive over but not today. He pulled in, parked haphazardly and, as always, patted the sculpture of the Goat outside the main door. Each year dozens of models of that year's Chinese Zodiac animal were displayed throughout Cleveland's AsiaTown. There were animals from several years outside Siam Café.

The Chinese zodiac, known as Sheng Xiao or Shu Xiang, features 12 animal signs in this order: Rat, Ox, Tiger, Rabbit, Dragon, Snake, Horse, Goat, Monkey, Rooster, Dog and Pig.

Ren had been patting the Goat since it was installed because it signified a year of promise and prosperity. It couldn't hurt, right?

His Vietnamese friends called it a sheep while his Korean buddy insisted it was a ram. But to Ren, the Zodiac's Chinese character yáng referred to both goats and sheep and in the south of China, where his roots were, it was more likely to be thought of as a goat while in the North they thought it was a sheep. Goat, ram or sheep he didn't want to miss out on the promised prosperity.

He entered the restaurant and spotted his friend Dick Jamieson, DJ to almost everyone, in a favorite booth in the back. It was by the live fish tanks and Ren and DJ liked it partly because the third member of their team was unnerved by the live fish, frogs and lobsters.

Even seated you could tell that DJ was tall and had probably played a lot of sports. He had jet black hair and more than one person had told him that he had the map of Ireland on his face, whatever that meant. DJ was pretty sure that "Jamieson" was a Scottish name, not Irish, but he took it as a compliment.

"What's up with you?" DJ asked as Ren approached at a rapid clip. "You look like you've seen a ghost."

Ren was breathing heavy from rushing in and asked "Where's Peggy? I don't want to have to tell this twice."

As if on cue, Peggy Powell strolled into the restaurant. She frowned when she saw where the guys had chosen to sit. "Gross!" she thought but she was determined to not let them get a rise out of her.

Peggy was about 5' 7" tall with a slender build. Her long brown hair was held together by a scrunchie as it cascaded down her back. Her green eyes were covered by enormous eyeglasses and for some reason she frequently put on a different pair that she grabbed from the large bag slung over her shoulder. The guys had been teasing her that the oversized purse that she always carried soon would have a life of its own.

The three may have had different physical appearances but they were best friends and business partners.

"Hurry up Peggy," DJ beckoned as she approached. "Ren looks like he's about to burst!"

"You'd burst too if you found out you were a murderer!" Ren did indeed explode.

Chapter 3 – The Present

"I've seen you kill a plate of Pad Thai but that doesn't make you a murderer," DJ joked. "Very funny Deej," Ren retorted and proceeded to tell them about what he found in the archives.

"So you resemble a murderer from decades ago." Peggy stated. "Why are you so upset?"

Ren was about to answer when the waiter arrived with their food. He figured his story could wait a few more minutes and he attacked the appetizer with gusto. They had ordered 6 pan fried pork dumplings and Ren was grabbing his second before the others had unfolded their napkins. DJ had his usual General Tso's Chicken and Peggy, who was an on-again-off-again vegan, had the sautéed spinach with garlic sauce.

"I guess you won't be smooching with anyone tonight Peggy with all that garlic sauce," DJ teased. Peggy blushed and retorted, "Wouldn't you like to know."

Both Ren and DJ considered Peggy to be like a little sister and while they teased her unmercifully sometime, woe be to someone else who gave her a hard time.

DJ had Sinh to Xoai, a delicious mango shake, Ren had a lychee boba (bubble) tea and Peggy had, well, a "Peggy". When the three were working on their Cultural Gardens project last year they were regulars at the Cultural Gardens Café where health-conscious Peggy always ordered the same green concoction. Ren and DJ had taken tentative sips of it once and declared it undrinkable. But Peggy kept ordering it till one day when the owner took their order he said "And a Peggy for you, right Miss?" The name stuck. Peggy blushed but was even more chagrined when the owner actually changed the name of the beverage to "Peggy" on the menu.

Ren had scarfed down his food and was sipping his bubble tea while the other two worked on theirs. He finally got to the cause of his concern. "I'm not upset that I look like a twin of the guy," he offered. "I'm mad because I think he was innocent. Somebody framed him!"

Chapter 4 – The Present

This pronouncement stopped the chopsticks halfway to DJ and Peggy's mouths. "Why do you say that?" DJ asked. "Many reasons" Ren replied. "From what I read, the evidence, if you can call it that, was clearly fabricated and he had a court appointed attorney who probably just wanted to get the case over. And I think he was railroaded because he was Chinese."

DJ and Peggy looked on thoughtfully and Ren added, "Plus nobody as good looking as me and him could be guilty!" and all three burst out laughing.

After they quieted down DJ said "Well there's not much we can do about a decades old court case. We can mention some of the prejudices the early immigrants faced in our project but that's about it, right?"

"Wrong" Ren answered. I think we should find the real murderer and get the case reopened and clear his name."

"How can we do that?" asked Peggy and the three sat in silence thinking. Suddenly Ren's eyes lit up and he said "There's only one person who can help us." After a brief pause, all three blurted out at the same time, "Margaret!"

Margaret Wong is a nationally and internationally renowned immigration lawyer with offices all over the country but her main office is in Cleveland. Located at East 32nd and Chester, Margaret W. Wong and Associates LLC was just on the border of the AsiaTown neighborhood of Cleveland.

Born in Hong Kong, Margaret came to the United States in 1969 on a student visa. She came with her sister Cecilia and the two of them had $187 to share.

Margaret worked as a waitress to pay her college and law school tuition. Another sister, Rose, and her brother George would follow later.

Her first stop in the States was Iowa where she attended an all girls' Catholic school which was run by nuns in the small town of Ottumwa. After she finished Jr. College she went on to Western Illinois University where she received her Bachelor's Degree in 1973.

Her sister Cecilia went to Syracuse and Margaret went to State University of New York, Buffalo and then on to law school.

She became one of the very first non U.S. citizens licensed to practice law both in New York and Ohio. She became a proud U.S. citizen.

Since starting her own firm in Cleveland, Margaret's company has become one of the most respected immigration law firms in the country. And her reputation has grown to the point that even the families of US presidents have sought her counsel.

Outside of all the accolades and awards, Margaret remained loyal and accessible to the Cleveland community and supported hundreds of ethnic events, organizations and publications. DJ, Ren and Peggy had all met Margaret many times and though at first intimidated, they grew to see her as a caring and generous person.

"One problem." Peggy pointed out. "Margaret is an immigration attorney not a murder defense attorney."

The trio discussed some options as they ordered another round of drinks and had some red bean ice cream. They concluded that while they were sure that the generous attorney would assist them they did not want to waste her time. So they would do as much legwork as they could and when they were sure, they would present their case to Margaret. So they did.

Chapter 5 – The Past

Bud Sweeney rode the streetcar down Superior Ave. jingling the few coins in his pocket. It had been a long day at work. James Francis Sweeney was nicknamed "Bud" as an infant when his aunt exclaimed in her Irish brogue that he was a "wee bud of a boy" and it became a lifelong nickname.

He was a Lieutenant in the Cleveland Fire Department. He had started out at #1 House on West 3rd and St Clair and then moved to #5 at 34th and St Clair. His Captain had recently moved him to the Arson Squad.

The promotion came suddenly when his predecessor was "reassigned" after a rash of murders in which the killer tried to cover up the evidence by setting fire to where the body was dumped. He missed the days of just being one of the guys but the rank and file respected him as one of their own. He was always the first to enter a burning building. Never a desk jockey, he still routinely shook off his clothes before heading home to knock off any cockroaches from burnt buildings.

For the third time he took the change from his pocket and counted. The total never changed. He was looking forward to a cold beer at Dana's at East 30th and Payne but he only had enough for a fishbowl or two of draft for himself. His father had taught him years ago that he should never enter a tavern if he could not offer his friends a drink. Bud was hoping that being a Thursday night the bar wouldn't be too crowded and maybe Dana, the owner/bartender, would let him add to his tab.

Bud had an hour or so to kill before he picked up his daughter at St. Columbkille's School on East 26th and Payne. She was staying after classes with her friends to practice their Irish dancing for an upcoming recital. The school wasn't that far from their home on East 32nd street but he felt better walking her home, especially in the evening. He didn't like how some of the neighborhood guys looked at the schoolgirls and made comments and whistled.

St. Columbkille Church, at the southeast corner of East 26th and Superior, was an impressive edifice. The school across the street on the north side of Superior was more ramshackle. The custodian had to fire up the boiler every day. There were only four classrooms with two grades in each classroom at a time. Four Ursuline nuns shared the teaching duties.

Fr. Arthur Gallagher was the Pastor and he was assisted by Fr. John Wilson. Fr. Wilson was adept at sign language so St. Columbkille became the center of the Catholic Diocese outreach to the deaf community. One of their Sunday Masses featured sign language interpreters.

The Church was built by and for the local Irish community. Different communities with Eastern European roots lived in the neighborhood and all had their own churches. There was St Peter's for the Germans, Immaculate Conception (called "The Mac") for the Irish near Superior and 42nd St., and a slew of others like St Jospahat on East 33rd for the Polish community, St Sava on East 36th for the Serbians, St George for the Syrian Orthodox and so on. The abundance of local churches and schools let families and kids walk to services and school.

Bud got off the streetcar at East 30th and started walking south from Superior to Payne to his usual haunt, Dana's. He opened the door and was dismayed at how crowded it was. He made his way to his usual stool and ordered a fishbowl of draft beer. He waved 'hello' to several and shouted "Hi Stash" to some guys at the other end of the bar. Three "Stashes" waved back.

Bud thought that every street seemed to have at least one "Stash." It had to be the most popular name in the neighborhood. Someone had told him once that "Stash" was short for the name "Stanislav" and was popular in the Slavic countries of Central and Eastern Europe. And around 30th and Payne in Cleveland he thought to himself.

He laughed to himself how the whole neighborhood had been calling a friend of his daughter's the wrong name for years. Everyone called her Milka Moya because that was what her mother always yelled from the porch to her. "Milka Moya" come home to dinner. "Milka Moya" do your homework.

Bud's daughter Pat and her friends assumed that "Milka Moya" was her preferred name so began calling her that. Soon the entire neighborhood did as well. Only years later did they learn that her name was actually "Millie" and that her mother, in her native language, was calling "My dear Millie" when she said "Milka Moya." Millie/Milka must have liked it because she never corrected them.

Bud turned to his buddy Seamus and pointed at his beer but miraculously Seamus declined the offer pointing at his own full glass and two shot glasses lined up as backups.

Much relieved, Bud fished for his pack of Pall Malls and put the pack and some matches on the bar thankful that his bar tab would not grow this night.

That prompted Marko Pavlovic to pull his usual stunt. He sidled up to Bud and asked "Hey Lieutenant, can I borrow a smoke?"

"Borrow?" Bud thought. Marko always had his hand out. He never seemed to have his own pack of cigarettes. Marko only smoked Pall Malls which was Bud's brand. Bud looked at the pack. Only two smokes remained. He sighed as he handed one to Marko knowing it would be a long night for him with only one cigarette left.

"How's your daughter doing Bud? She's growing up fast isn't she?" Marko leered. Bud leapt off the bar stool and stood nose to nose with Marko. "Don't you ever talk about or look at or even think about my daughter ever again, you hear me?" Marko nervously backed away with hands extended to his side. "Sure Bud I was just asking," he lied.

Bud stood staring for a while and then returned to his bar stool. His buddy Seamus said "You look bad Bud. I think you need a shot." He signaled Dana with 2 fingers and the bartender brought over a bottle of Old Crow and 2 shot glasses.

"Did you hit the number Seamus? How come you are so flush?" Bud asked. His friend just smiled and lifted his glass and toasted "Sláinte" which means "health" in Irish and Scottish Gaelic.

Bud lifted the Old Crow and poured it down. It burned but it was a soothing, familiar burn. He felt bad about sitting in the bar drinking but it had been a rough day. As the new Lieutenant in the Arson Squad of the Cleveland Fire Department he had a lot on his mind.

Despite the noisy patrons, Dana answered the ringing telephone and handed it to Bud. "I'm not here," mouthed Bud but Dana said, "It's not your wife."

Bud picked up the phone and Chief Lloyd McKenna got right to the point. "There's been another one."

Chapter 6 – The Past

Bud knew what the Chief meant. There had been two murders in Chinatown in recent weeks and each time the body was found smoldering from a fire. Cleveland's Chinatown was primarily along Rockwell Ave. with restaurants like Shanghai Restaurant, the Three Sisters and the Golden Coins along with the Ming Tsang Grocery Store.

The Chinese were the first Asian group to come to Cleveland with a significant number coming in the late 1800s. Many Chinese, like so many others, were lured to California because of the Gold Rush of 1848–1855. More came because of large labor projects such as the building of the first transcontinental railroad. When the gold and jobs dried up and anti-Chinese sentiment and violence grew, many move eastward to places like Cleveland, Ohio.

The first Chinatown in Cleveland was actually around Public Square at the center of the city. Many settled in an area along Lakeside and St. Clair along Ontario Street.

Won Kee opened Cleveland's first Chinese restaurant on East 12th and Ontario in 1895. Others, like the Golden Dragon, soon followed mostly on the west side of Public Square. Not only did they provide good and familiar food they were a safe gathering place for immigrants.

The 1910 Census showed that a grand total of eleven Chinese lived in the Public Square area – of those, eight said they had originally been in California.

Most of these early immigrants had some education and work experience. They typically opened small service businesses such as laundries, restaurants, groceries and clothing stores. These were run by men because women weren't allowed to come yet. So there were very few children as well.

The Old Stone Church on Public Square became a focal point for the community. Two nuns worked for three decades with the Chinese community and taught themselves a working knowledge of Cantonese. In 1911, Dr. Sun Yat-sen, the founder of the Chinese Revolution, came to Cleveland and spoke at the Church.

The Golden Dragon Restaurant on Public Square hosted meetings to support and raise funds for Dr. Sun Yat-sen's movement to overthrow the rulers of the Qing (Ching) Dynasty. The 1911 Revolution successfully ended China's last imperial dynasty and the Republic of China was founded and officially proclaimed on January 1, 1912.

Ren's research had found that in February 1912 there was a celebration at the Old Stone Church and a telegram of congratulations was sent in the name of the Chinese residents to Dr. Sun, the new president of the Chinese Republic.

By the 1920's there were about 700 Chinese males in Cleveland. Most were immigrants from the southern Cantonese province of Guangdong who had first come to the West Coast of the US. Then more came from central China, Hong Kong and Taiwan.

The Cleveland Chinese Benevolent Association hosted an annual Chinese Picnic and large plots of land were bought at the West Park Cemetery so Chinese people could have a place to be buried together as a community.

With time, Cleveland's Chinatown moved eastward and centered along Rockwell Ave. between East 21st and 24th streets, not far from the Irish, Germans, Serbians and others around East 30th and Payne.

Bud liked the neighborhood and the variety of his neighbors. Sure, the different groups made fun of each other but it was mostly in a friendly way. It was usually about a group being stingy or losing a sporting event. It was not uncommon for someone to refer to a stingy person as still having their First Communion money.

Bud Sweeney wasn't thinking about the neighborhood's ethnic diversity or the history of Chinese immigration to Cleveland. His only concern was the rash of deadly arsons in his city.

Chapter 7 – The Past

Lieutenant Sweeney nursed his fishbowl of beer and thought back to the recent events. He and Chief McKenna were pretty sure that the first victim was a drifter, someone who had hopped off the railroad cars that ran just south of Lake Erie. Bud and his engine company had been called when someone spotted smoke coming from the area where hobos gathered. When the firetruck arrived they moved quickly to douse the flames coming from a crude wooden lean-to. As the fire died they spotted the body.

They radioed Cleveland Police and Bud didn't need his years of training in arson to tell Chief McKenna the cause of the fire. Anyone with a nose could smell the gasoline.

There was also a burnt rat that almost looked placed on the victim's body. It must have crawled up there before it died. In any case it was disgusting and Bud wondered what had happened to this poor man to end up burned in a shanty with a dead rat.

His train of thought was broken when the bar door squeaked open and a pathetic figure ambled in. Dorothy Tomcho was carrying two large bags from Stanley's grocery store down the road at 34th and Payne Ave. She bought items on credit at Stanley's and then sold them for a profit to the patrons of Dana's and a few other bars in the neighborhood. Her daughter Anna Catherine (Anna Cat to everyone but her mother who called her Annie) carried another bag.

Dorothy looked like she was in her 40s but in reality she had Anna Cat when she was only 15. She had had a rough life since the scandal of giving birth as an unwed teen but she did her best to be a good mother for Anna Cat who was her whole world.

Anna Cat was just 12 years old and extremely shy. Her mother worried about her because she was already drawing unwanted attention from men for her blossoming good looks. She was already taller than most of the boys in her school class. She had the same black hair as her mother and when they both wore it in ponytails they could have passed for sisters.

Dorothy made sure that both she and her daughter wore baggy, unfashionable clothes and avoided eye contact or non-business conversation with boys or men. She also reminded the creeps that Anna Cat was only 12 whenever they got too fresh.

Like many times before, some of the unsavory characters in the bar started to give Dorothy, and Anna Cat, a hard time. Marko and his look-alike brother Miro were the crudest. One look from Bud Sweeney calmed them down some. Nobody wanted to mess with the Lieutenant who was strong and chiseled from his training and work as a fireman.

Miro was a year younger than his brother but looked almost identical except he didn't smoke and Marko seemed to always have a cigarette – bummed from someone else usually - hanging from his lips.

Dorothy sold a few apples and a pie to Seamus and the mother and daughter hurried out of the bar. Bud was wondering where Seamus was coming up with the money. Seamus was a good guy, working on the docks where the Cuyahoga River merged into Lake Erie. It was a rough job but Seamus was young and strong.

He had come from Ireland a few years before and settled with some cousins in the local St. Columbkille's Parish where he met Bud and his family. Seamus, like so many other Irish immigrants to Cleveland was originally from County Mayo on the west coast of Ireland. In particular, he was from Achill

Island, the largest of the Irish Isles. Achill was just off the west coast of Ireland in County Mayo. Only a few thousand people lived on the island but there were thousands more in Cleveland who had roots there.

The Sweeneys, Bud's family, were one of the few Irish in Cleveland not from Achill or even County Mayo. They were from County Monaghan, a couple hours drive east in Ireland.

Bud was glad that there were people like Seamus who hung out at Dana's. He was always concerned what might be happening when he wasn't around. Some of the regulars, especially Marko and Miro, were just mean, especially when they were drinking.

Dana, the owner, was a good guy but he was also a businessman and the money that came in from the lowlifes was just as needed as from the others. He pulled out the baseball bat he kept behind the bar only in extreme circumstances.

As Bud's hand searched his empty pockets he wondered how the bad guys always seemed to have money, even without regular jobs.

He wasn't too concerned about Miro Pavlovic who was basically just a mooch and a loudmouth but his brother Marko was another story. He had something bad to say about everyone – everyone weaker than him at least.

Marko started calling Sammy, the neighborhood teen with the limp, "Flash" and sadly the name stuck. They constantly poked fun at him and set him up with hurtful pranks. Sammy had to try and smile and take it.

For some reason Marko named the young man with the learning disabilities "Peanuts Popcorn Bobbie." Nobody knew why except to make Bobbie feel small and Marko feel big.

Bud knew that Marko and Miro saved their worst treatment for people of different ethnic backgrounds – especially the Chinese. So he was on edge when Henry Fong entered the bar with a delivery of food from his family's restaurant, Chin's.

Chapter 8 – The Past

Marko and Miro Pavlovic had only moved into the neighborhood a few years ago. They had been chased out of their previous home for being a nuisance. Though Marko was a year older, he and Miro could have been twins. They were about 5' 10" tall and wiry. They had dark eyes and a wisp of moustache under broad noses. Marko's teeth were more yellow due to his chain smoking but other than that they were almost indistinguishable.

They had both been in trouble in high school for bullying, petty theft and the like but it wasn't until Marko started paying too much attention to a young Lithuanian girl that things got serious.

The St Clair neighborhood in the East 60's and 70's was a hodgepodge of immigrants of Croatian, Lithuanian, Serbian, Slovenian, Polish and other heritages. The families were hard-working, religious and protective of their families. So when Romas Gudenas caught Marko Pavlovic sniffing around his pre-teen daughter he gave him a well-deserved warning – with both fists – right outside St. Vitus, the Slovenian Church near East 60th and St. Clair Ave.

This public reprimand both embarrassed and infuriated Marko and he was never the same. His previous bullying evolved into outright assaults and the petty thefts became robberies. His brother Miro and a few other losers were more than happy to take part in the action.

When Miro and Marko were fired from their factory jobs they blamed the immigrant newcomers who replaced them even though the cause of Marko's termination was for bothering the girls in the office and Miro rarely showing up for work on time.

Since then, anyone who looked different or was weak was a likely target for their abuse. The protective neighborhood fathers were making their activities increasingly difficult so they moved. They rented a house on East 31st between Payne and Perkins and moved in. It was just a short walk to East 30th and Payne where they found their new hangout, Dana's Bar.

They both applied for work at the Pepsi plant at East 34th between Chester and Perkins but after less than a week they were fired.

Soon they hooked up with some other lowlifes at the bar and started their harassment again. There were a lot of targets like the kid Sammy with the limp, that crazy kid Bobbie and others. They didn't like Irish immigrants either but were smart enough not to mess with the Irish fireman or the longshoreman Seamus. Marko was always eager to watch the young Irish girls walk home from St. Columbkille's school down the street but he knew not to go too far. He imagined that the Irish fireman would be even tougher on him than that Lithuanian dad had been in the old neighborhood.

They made enough money from odd jobs or robbing places, like Stanley's Delicatessen, to get by. And it was a lot of fun harassing that Chinaman kid with the ponytail or the bag lady and her daughter and others.

Chapter 9 – The Past

As soon as Marko noticed Henry Fong's arrival he started in on him. He pulled his eyes apart in a slant and said in a sing-song voice, "Chin Chin Chinaman sitting on a fence, trying to make a dollar out of fifteen cents." Henry just nodded and smiled and handed the food over to Dana at the bar. Marko and his crew continued with a few more racist comments until Bud and Seamus and a few others stood up and told them to shut up.

Bud and Seamus's cousins had lived through the "No Irish need apply" days when their families first came over from Ireland so they were not going to allow similar treatment to others. Besides, Bud and Henry had become friends over the years and when he had saved up enough he would take his family to Chin's for a great meal of new, exotic foods like fried rice, egg rolls and something called chop suey.

Bud had become friends with two Chinese boxers – Eddie Woo and Georgie Toy – who were Gold Gloves champions at their local gym. Eddie Woo was half Chinese and half Slovenian which made him a perfect representative of the diverse neighborhood.

Gold Gloves events were very popular and every school seemed to have a program. Bud's eldest son Jim had had some epic battles with Sam Coso, a Serbian teen from the neighborhood. They fought hard but once they left the ring, they were great friends.

Bud was also friends with David Shuguchi whose family had moved to the corner of East 32nd and Perkins right after the war. Dave was 5' 10" and was quarterback at East High School. East High School, home of the Blue Bombers, was at East 79th and Superior in Cleveland's Hough neighborhood. Opposing players were often surprised to learn that the star player from that neighborhood's school was Japanese.

When they were boxing or playing football or just doing calisthenics, the race of his buddies never mattered to Bud. They were just guys. That's how he felt about Henry too.

Bud had confided to Henry that he might be left alone more if he didn't wear exaggerated and stereotypical clothes. Henry always wore a jacket with a dragon on it and a conical bamboo hat over his ponytail as he pedaled his bicycle through the neighborhood making deliveries. Even the bike with its basket was painted with dragons.

Henry was still a teenager but a smart businessman. He explained that this was part of their sales approach. Many people wanted the experience of "a real live Chinaman" delivering their food. He could take some teasing as long as the orders kept coming. It was when it went beyond teasing that he became concerned.

Bud had to leave to walk his daughter home but he made sure that Henry was pedaling away before he said goodnight and headed to Saint Columbkille Church and School on the corner of Superior and East 26th Street.

His daughter Patricia was waiting for him with a group of other young girls in their school uniforms. She danced up to him, showing off a newly learned step. Her excited greeting and hug and non-stop tales of her day made him forget about Marko, Miro and the latest arson murder. At least for a while.

Chapter 10 – The Past

Bud sat down with his family for a late supper. They had lived in several houses on East 32nd Street between Payne and Perkins over the years. Bud's wife Helen worked at Jack and Heintz, a local manufacturing plant. Every day she walked down East 32nd to Payne Ave. to catch a bus to work.

Bill Jack and Ralph Heintz formed Jack & Heintz in 1940 in Palo Alto, California. Soon after that they moved their company to Cleveland and made airplane parts. They received a military contract to produce airplane starters for the war effort. By 1944, Jack and Heintz employed over 8700 workers which included several thousand women like Helen Sweeney.

When the war ended, however, the lucrative military contracts dried up and they continued to produce airplane parts but also began making electric motors. In 1961 they were merged into Siegler Corp. and became focused primarily on aerospace.

Though working full-time, Helen still managed to come up with delicious meals from her German and Austrian heritage like chicken paprikash and stuffed cabbage. Beside Patricia, they had two boys; the studious Jim and the more carefree youngest, Terry.

They had a good life with family, church and school nearby. Helen's mother Marie, who everyone called Gram, had come from Austria at age sixteen and married John. Together they had eleven children and lots of grandkids but somehow they all fit in the small house on East 43rd and Superior for holidays and celebrations.

To Pat, Jim and Terry and their cousins, Gram's house was magical. The kids had never seen a cigar tree before like the one in front of Gram's house. The (non-edible) fruit was 7 inches or more and shaped and colored like a cigar. Hundreds would hang from the tree and when they turned brown in the fall it looked like a tree of cigars.

Gram's house had lots of interesting and fun features such as the cellar door around the side that you could climb over. But it was Christmas that they always remembered. As they drove by the house in later years they marveled that despite how small the house appeared there was always the biggest Christmas tree in the world in the family room.

Before presents could be opened on Christmas Eve each year the family gathered around the huge tree, knelt down, and said a family rosary always saying extra prayers for those in the armed services. It was not uncommon for some of the men to sneak off during the prayers to the kitchen where everybody had brought a bottle of their favorite booze. Then the gifts were opened under the massive tree.

Bud was grateful for such family traditions and as he looked around the dinner table was thankful for his wife and three kids but he had seen a dark side of humanity and didn't know how he could protect them from it. His holiday musings were interrupted when he heard the yelling.

Bud jumped up, knocking over his coffee cup in the process. Helen and the kids looked at him unbelievingly and then started laughing. "It's just the Paper Rex man, Dad," Pat said. The Paper Rex man was a familiar figure in the neighborhood. He went up and down the streets pulling a cart yelling "Paper, rags".

When people had paper or rags or pots, pans, bottles and anything else he might buy they would go outside and negotiate with the Paper Rex man.

The heavy Jewish accent of the man made the "paper, rags" cries sound like "Paper Rex" so that is what he was called. Sometimes he had an old wrinkled horse pulling the cart so the kids would gather around to see the horse and maybe feed him a carrot. All five Sweeneys, and most of the neighbors, went outside to see the excitement.

A few years ago, an exasperated Helen approached the Paper Rex man and asked "Will you take these 3 bad kids?" He had replied, "I won't take them but I'll take you." Ever since, Bud tried to be around when the man came by.

They didn't have anything to buy or sell that evening but it became a social gathering with the neighbors. Bud saw his friend Stanley rounding the corner from Payne to his house on East 32nd.

Stanley was owner of Stanley's Grocery Store and Deli on 34th and Payne. He charged up to Bud and began venting. Some in the closely knit neighborhood of immigrants were intimidated by the Police so they used Bud as their complaint department. After all, he was a fireman and was there to help people. Plus, he had the uniform.

When he spotted Helen, Stanley stopped and tipped his hat. "Evening Mrs. Sweeney," he said and then steered Bud over by a tree. "It's getting out of hand," he complained. "What is?"

Bud asked. "Marko and Miro and their bunch of goons. They got a snootful of booze at Dana's and then came up to my store and just took whatever they wanted. And they made a mess of everything too. Third time this month. Marko even took a carton of Pall Malls! I tried to stop them but Miro just pushed me and laughed."

Bud was concerned. He knew that before he came to this country Stanley had been in the army. He was a tough cookie. Just because he was older now didn't mean he wasn't still a crack shot with his gun. "I tell you Bud," Stanley said, "Somebody should take care of Marko and his brother once and for all."

Chapter 11 – The Past

Bud lit up his last Pall Mall of the day and tried to calm Stanley down. "Don't do anything stupid Stanley. You have too much to lose," he offered. "I won't – yet," replied Stanley "but somebody should. They are a menace in this neighborhood." He tipped his hat goodnight to Mrs. Sweeney and headed back to his store which was also his home.

An elderly man wearing a white smock ambled up to Bud. Dr. Hartman was the neighborhood dentist and had his office upstairs from the Yale drugstore on the SE corner of East 32nd and Payne. The drugstore and Stanley's store were anchors of the community along with Bill Welker's meat market and Jim Sinnett's candy and ice cream store. Dr. Hartman said, "I overheard you talking about those thugs with Stanley. I've seen them casing my place several times. I'm worried they may be after my Lidocaine or Nitrous Oxide." When Bud looked puzzled he said, "You know it as Laughing Gas. The police should do something."

Bud repeated the explanation that he had been forced to give to so many people lately. "Unfortunately, the police can't do anything until a crime has actually been committed." "I know," agreed the dentist, "But we all know something bad is going to happen. If the police can't do anything, maybe somebody else should."

The men shook hands and Bud called to the kids to come inside and the family laughed and joked – everyone talking at once it seemed – till they settled in for bed. Pat dreamt of her Irish dance recital, Jim of getting an A on his test and Terry about becoming a fireman like his dad.

The next few days were busy ones as the arson investigations intensified. Bud barely had enough energy to get home to bed each night let alone stop for a drink at Dana's.

Finally they caught a break. It was looking like a drifter was responsible for the recent arsons and murders. Chief McKenna told him he had done a good job and gave him a $5 bonus! Bud decided to celebrate with a few coins from that bonus at Dana's and to repay Seamus for the drinks. The rest would go to next month's rent so they wouldn't have to move to the Rat House.

The Rat House was on East 32nd Street between Perkins and Payne. The residents of the street were all on monthly rental agreements and when hard times hit and they couldn't afford the rent they would move into the Rat House down the street which had very minimal rent.

The place was well named because it seems that rats were the true owners of the house. It was always sad to see a neighbor family carting their belongings to the rat house. It was even worse when it was your family under the pitying eyes of the entire street. Even though both he and his wife Helen worked, they had three kids and there was always an unexpected expense.

Pat was a teen now and needed dresses for her Irish dancing. It wouldn't be too many years until they would be expected to pay for her wedding. Jim was so smart – Bud knew he was going to go to college someday if they could afford it. Terry was still too young to know what the future held for him but Bud expected it to be expensive as well. But first things first. He had to keep them out of the Rat House and he needed a beer.

When he got to Dana's he couldn't believe his eyes. Marko and Miro and about 6 of their cronies were in a circle and they were pushing "Flash" and "Peanuts Popcorn Bobbie" back and forth. Dana was yelling at them to stop but they ignored him, even when he grabbed the baseball bat from behind the bar.

As Bud entered, Miro gave an extra hard shove to the poor boy with the bad leg. Sammy fell down and Miro jumped on top of him. Bobbie cowered in a corner. The thugs all laughed until they saw Bud enter. He was an impressive sight in his uniform. Bud went up to Miro and pulled him off the young man. He squared off with Marko and told him if he wanted to mess with someone he should mess with him. Marko just laughed and said "Let's get out of this dump" and led his crew outside.

Bud helped Sammy up and checked on Bobbie. Sammy sobbed, "Somebody has to do something about Marko and Miro. I can't take it anymore." Bobbie just rocked back and forth hugging his knees. Dana came from around the bar to pick up chairs and clean up. "I tell you Bud," he said, "there's something going on with Marko. He's getting worse and worse and somebody has to do something about it. Before he was just scaring away my customers but now him and his brother are manhandling them and busting up the place. I was this close to using my bat on him and teaching him a permanent lesson."

"The worst thing is," he continued, "when Dorothy and Anna Cat came in yesterday he said something perverted to Anna Cat and she turned and buried her face in her mother's arms. Miro and the others laughed at the rejection so Marko lashed out and dumped their groceries all over and screamed at them. Anna Cat looked like she had seen a ghost – she was petrified.

Dorothy tried to pick up some of the groceries but he kept kicking them away and laughing when she bent over. He made some obscene comments as Dorothy and Anna Cat bent over to pick up the groceries and finally Dorothy and her daughter left in tears. Anna Cat had a horrified expression. The poor kid."

Bud felt terrible for the hard working mother and her young daughter. He promised Dana he would talk to a Cleveland PD friend the next day. Marko and Miro had to be stopped before they went too far. But it was too late.

Chapter 12 – The Past

Henry Fong was tired. It wasn't easy pedaling that bicycle around town delivering his family's foods but he preferred that to working in the restaurant. He didn't like when the weather was bad, as it often was in Cleveland, but the sunny days made up for it. He also didn't like the very few customers who treated him badly and seemed to hate him because of his Chinese heritage. He didn't get it. There were people from a lot of nationalities around their restaurant – German, Irish, Serbian, Lithuanian, Polish, Croatian and more - and most were very friendly and nice. Only a few were nasty.

Some people were a little concerned about trying the "foreign" food but they liked it once they did. He didn't have the heart to tell them that authentic Chinese cooking was nothing like what they were serving.   He knew his relatives in China were not eating dishes like sweet and sour chicken.

His parents were very protective and always cautioned him to be careful when making deliveries. Of course they didn't want him to get hurt but they were also concerned about the food and payments. Every dollar was important to this family owned business.

That's why they were excited the next day when they received a huge $15 order for delivery! They began preparing the "Chinese-American" food as they called it and told Henry to get ready. Henry was excited too until he saw the address for the delivery. It was Dana's Bar. He hoped that the order was for the nice fireman Lieutenant Sweeney or someone and not those bullies who hung out there.

Henry loaded up the bicycle basket and started pedaling to 30th and Payne. He pulled up next to the bar and engaged the kickstand on his bike. He started unloading the basket full of the food order when he felt the first blow. He saw Marko and Miro Pavlovic with their friends circling him and they began to throw punches and kicks. Henry tried to fight back but there were too many of them. He finally had to cover up and absorb the punishment as best he could.

It was obvious that Marko was the ringleader. He was calling Henry every racist name in the book and while Miro and the others were pushing or punching him, Marko was kicking as well. At least he thought it was Marko. Without a cigarette dangling from one of their mouths it was hard to distinguish. Especially during a beating.

Finally the pummeling stopped and he looked up from the ground to see Marko and the others taking the food from his basket and laughing. They held him as Marko checked his jacket pockets and took the few dollars he had with him that might have been needed to make change.

They called him names and laughed and started to walk away but Marko turned around and came toward him – with a knife! Henry thought this might be the end but Marko went over to his bicycle and slashed his tires. Then he turned toward Henry.

Henry was physically beaten and his food and money stolen and bicycle ruined but what happened next was the ultimate indignity.

Henry, like other males in his family, wore a traditional ponytail. It was not what was known as the Manchu queue where men shaved the front half of their head, leaving a bare forehead and the rest of the hair gathered up and plaited into a long braid that hangs down the back. But it was a standard ponytail that was a family tradition and meant a lot to the Fong family.

Marko approached Henry and as the others held him down, he took the knife and cut off Henry's ponytail. He laughed and threw it in the street as they walked away saying he didn't want to touch the dirty Chinese hair.

Henry was unable to stand for a few minutes but once he could, he swore to himself that he would have revenge.

Chapter 13 – The Past

All three Cleveland daily newspapers, (The News, Press and Plain Dealer) had a variation of the same headline – "Local Man Murdered, Chinaman Arrested".

The body of Marko Pavlovic had been found near the train tracks where the other murders had taken place. Attempts had been made to burn the body like the other victims. There was a dead rat near the body, just like the others. A crumpled pack of Pall Malls was nearby.

Witnesses had come forward and told the police that the Chinese delivery boy had been in a fight with the "victim" and had sworn revenge. Other witnesses had seen Henry that night by the tracks near Marko's body. The police soon found the bruised Henry Fong nursing his wounds at his family's restaurant and arrested him for murder.

"I didn't do anything!" Henry cried as they handcuffed him. "They beat me up, stole everything and cut my bicycle tires. They are the bad guys!"

"Tell it to the judge," an officer advised Henry. His family pleaded in a combination of English and Cantonese as they took Henry away. Henry was taken to the police station on East 20th and Payne and placed in a cell. The family didn't know what to do. They didn't have the connections, or money, for a lawyer. They closed up the restaurant and hurried to the police station.

Desk Sergeant Ken Morley was not in the mood to coddle a probable murderer. "These people come here and then they kill upstanding citizens," he thought to himself. His perspective mellowed as he saw the pain in the family. He explained the concept of bail to them but told them it was probably not going to be allowed for a murder charge. Plus it was very expensive. After some more tears and pleading he decided to help – not the murderer, but the devastated family.

He knew of a few lawyers who had got themselves into trouble over the years who weren't prosecuted as a "professional courtesy." It was understood that they would quietly pay off their debt to society by being available to occasionally take on unpopular cases for no charge. He dialed the rotary telephone on his desk and when it was answered he said, "Johnson? It's Morley. I need you down at the 3rd District. Now."

The Third District police building was on the north side of Payne Ave at East 20th and it was huge. It had an interesting history. In 1931, Eliot Ness was a prohibition agent in Chicago. A member of Al Capone's gang promised Ness that he would receive $2,000 every week (almost $40,000 today) if he ignored their bootlegging activities. Ness turned down that bribe and subsequent attempts to bribe or intimidate him and his agents. This earned them the nickname The Untouchables.

In December 1935, Cleveland mayor Harold H. Burton hired Ness as the city's Safety Director. That put Ness in charge of both the police and fire departments. When Eliot Ness reorganized the police department in 1938, he transitioned the force from what had been eighteen precincts into five, larger districts, which were further divided into 32 zones. The newly formed Third District covered the territory east of the Cuyahoga River to about E. 63rd Street and north of Union Avenue, SE and was headquartered at CPD Central Station, at 2001 Payne Avenue. This included Cleveland's Chinatown.

Chapter 14 – The Past

Attorney Jack Johnson was not happy to be called down to the 3rd. He had already had a few drinks and wondered when his "debt to society" would finally be paid off. He was less happy when Sergeant Morley explained the situation and pointed out the anxious family members. "Great," he thought "a bunch of Chinamen who can barely speak English."

He forced a compassionate visage and met the family telling them he would do whatever he could. It worked. They seemed somewhat relieved and he was soon out the door and headed back to Mitzi Jerman's Café at 38th and St. Clair.

He wasn't in the best shape the next morning after too much drinking at Mitzi's as he met with the prosecutor, the arresting officers and the man who found the body. The evidence was overwhelming. As he expected this was clearly a case of a Chinaman who couldn't fit in to American society and decided to take it out on someone else. He made a mental note to tell Morley that this made them even for his "community service."

When he finally met with Henry Fong in a dingy cell in the back of the building his suspicions were confirmed. The murderer was disheveled and bruised. Probably got in a lot of fights. He had some kind of funny hair that he must have cut himself. "This won't take long," he thought. "Mr. Fong," he introduced himself, "I'm attorney Jack Johnson and I've been assigned to your case. Why did you kill all those men?"

Henry Fong was shocked. "What!" he exclaimed. "I didn't kill anyone. Those guys beat me half to death and as soon as I could I made my way home." Attorney Johnson shook his head from side to side. "Tell the truth – I am your lawyer. There is just too much evidence against you". "What evidence?" Henry asked incredulously.

"Come on Mr. Fong," the attorney replied. "They found your bicycle there – with all the dragons on it. Nobody else has a bike like that. After you fought with the victim you followed him on your bike and killed him, didn't you?"

"No!" Henry exploded. "They cut the tires on my bike. I couldn't ride it so I left it there and walked home."

"What about the other people you killed? You tried to burn their bodies just like you tried to burn Mr. Pavlovic, right Mr. Fong?" the lawyer asked.

50

Henry Fong felt he was in a nightmare. He had been jumped and beaten and robbed and now he was being blamed for multiple murders? This couldn't be real. He stared blankly and then asked, "How is my family doing? Can I see them?"

"Look, Mr. Fong," the lawyer explained. "There are witnesses and lots of evidence against you. You claim to care about your family. If you continue to lie there will be a trial and your family will have to sit in court every day and hear about the heinous things you have done. Why don't you just admit it and not put your family through all that pain and shame?"

"One other thing, Mr. Fong," the lawyer explained. "If we go to trial you will be charged with all of the murders. You will be found guilty and you will face the death penalty. Your family will have to go through all that. Is that what you want?"

Henry couldn't respond. If this was a nightmare he prayed to wake up. His mind went blank as the lawyer droned on. He managed to hear the lawyer say "If you plead guilty I think I can get the sentence reduced to life in prison. Your family could still visit you." Attorney Johnson knew he had struck a nerve with the family argument and kept pushing it.

"What's it going to be Mr. Fong?" he asked "I don't have all day."

Chapter 15 – The Present

Ren and DJ and Peggy had been called a modern Mod Squad after they solved the series of murders in the Cleveland Cultural Gardens last year. None of the three knew what the reference meant but after binge watching episodes of the show on YouTube they were flattered.

The Mod Squad was a crime series that aired on ABC from 1968 to 1973. Instead of the traditional police in suits like in Dragnet with Detective Joe Friday stating "Just the facts, ma'am" the investigators of The Mod Squad were an unlikely trio and promoted as "One black, one white, one blonde." They were supposed to appeal to the counterculture of the times in contrast to the conservative police officers in other shows.

Long-haired Pete was evicted from his wealthy parents' Beverly Hills home and arrested for stealing a car. Lincoln Hayes, better known as Linc, was an African-American who had been arrested in the Watts riots in Los Angeles. The third member was Julie Barnes who was a flower child and exemplified all the characteristics of a hippie girl of that time.

DJ, Ren and Peggy did not share any of the characteristics of the original Mod Squad but they too were an unlikely trio that ended up involved in murder cases so the name stuck.

It was never their intention to solve crimes but everything changed last summer. Dick "DJ" Jamieson and his friends and colleagues Ren Wu and Peggy Powell were in the Cleveland Cultural Gardens working on a project that they hoped would put their startup company on the map – and bring in some much-needed income. The trio had a variety of complementary skills and after years of using those skills for various volunteer projects around Cleveland they decided to start their own company.

Dick Jamieson had been called DJ since he was born. He was 6'2 with jet black hair and a square jawline. He seemed to always have a five-o'clock shadow. His powerful physique harkened back to what he called his "jock days" in high school and college. A seeming oxymoron, DJ's athletic prowess did not interfere with his logical mind that pursued physics, math and, of course, technology.

Peggy Powell was the "little sister" to the guys. She had been extremely shy all her life, preferring to spend her time in nature looking at plants or sketching in her notebook to more typical pursuits. After working on several volunteer projects around town with the guys she began to trust them and opened up a little. She was still prone to blushing profusely when they teased her but she was working on it.

With all her time in nature she was very sensitive to pollen and ragweed and the like so she had abandoned her contact lenses for a plethora of eyeglasses. To the guys she seemed to always be digging through her humongous purse to find just the right pair of glasses for the occasion.

When a mean girl had called her Mr. Magoo when Peggy was sporting a particularly large pair of glasses they had to Google the reference. When they saw that it was insulting, the guys jumped to her defense. They could tease her as much as they wanted, they reasoned, but nobody else could. Peggy always acted bothered and said she could take care of herself but inwardly she was very appreciative of her "big brothers."

The third member of the Mod Squad was Ren Wu who had been DJ's best friend for years. From appearances one might think that Ren was an easier target than the powerful DJ but Ren was a master of martial arts. He was also a gadget guru and film producer and always looking for the next thing. If there was a new gadget released, Ren would be all over it.

His willingness to take chances to get just the right movie shot earned him the nickname Reckless Ren. He was of Chinese heritage and looked the part, resembling a young Bruce Lee. Fluent in several languages, Ren enjoyed when people guessed his first language to be Chinese. It was actually Spanish because he was raised in Panama by his diplomat parents. His fan and feature films were beginning to garner national attention.

The three had met while volunteering on several different projects and soon saw that their complimentary skills made them a productive team. After a few trial runs they decided to formalize their relationship and start a business.

Theirs was a classic case of working "in" the business instead of "on" it and income was scarce. So when they met a Cleveland University professor who offered to back a summer long project they jumped at the chance. And with the subject of the project being one of their favorite places, the Cleveland Cultural Gardens, they were ecstatic. Little did they know the joy would not last as the project would lead them into a web of danger and murder and earn them the nickname "The Mod Squad."

Chapter 16 – The Present

It was Ren's idea to create a documentary on the rise of Cleveland's Chinatown and AsiaTown. He had learned that the Chinese were the first Asian group to come to Cleveland with most being immigrants from the southern Cantonese province of Guangdong. Guangdong was the first Chinese port to be regularly visited by European traders, who called it Canton. Many of the Chinese immigrants to Cleveland had first come to the West Coast of the US and then moved inland. Over the years, more came from central China, Hong Kong and Taiwan but the Cantonese were still the largest group.

About 60 miles south of Cleveland is the city of Canton, Ohio. Canton was founded in 1805 by Bezaleel Wells, a surveyor from Maryland. He was an admirer of Captain John O'Donnell, an Irish merchant marine with the British East India Company. O'Donnell named his estate in Maryland after Canton, China as he had been the first person to transport goods from there to Baltimore. So Wells called it Canton. The trio, like everyone else, called it CANton with the accent of the first syllable as opposed to the more Chinese pronunciation of CanTON. Cantonese restaurants and speakers were still found throughout Cleveland.

In her research, Peggy found out that Canton was the home of William McKinley, the 25th president of the United States, for most of his life. DJ was a frequent visitor to the NFL Football Hall of Fame in Canton and their research turned up a lot of other notables from Canton such as Macy Gray, The O'Jays, Marilyn Manson, Jack Paar, Boz Scaggs, Thurman Munson, Marion Motley and others. Not bad for a city with about 70,000 residents.

About sixty miles to the north in Cleveland, restaurants and laundries had gathered along Rockwell Ave. between East 21st and 24th forming Cleveland's Chinatown. It was still primarily Cantonese but was becoming more diverse as people came from Shanghai and other cities of China.

Ren was proud that he was fluent in both Mandarin and Cantonese (along with Spanish and English). He also enjoyed messing with Peggy and DJ about the languages. When Peggy would say, "Gong hei fat choy" to wish him a happy Chinese New Year he would correct her saying the proper greeting was "Xīnnián kuàilè." A dejected Peggy would pout until Ren laughed and told her the first greeting was Cantonese and the second was Mandarin but both sentiments were appreciated.

Both Peggy and DJ were trying to learn Mandarin from Ren but were having trouble with the 5 tones. DJ could not believe that if he said the word "ma" for example with one tone it meant "mother" but if he said it in another tone it meant "horse!" DJ made a mental note to never use that word lest he accidentally call his mother a horse.

When DJ complained how hard the language is to learn, Ren would quote Jackie Chan who supposedly complained about the English language saying, "Read and lead rhyme and read and lead rhyme but read and lead don't rhyme and neither do read and lead."

Other Asians came to Cleveland after the Chinese. Japanese immigrants came after WWII and were made much more welcome than they had been on the West Coast. There, the War Relocation Authority had moved them from their homes to internment camps during World War II.

After the December 1941 attack on Pearl Harbor, President Franklin D. Roosevelt authorized the creation of zones from which certain persons could be excluded if they posed a threat to national security. Since people of Japanese ancestry were considered a threat of espionage after the Pearl Harbor attack, all of California and parts of Washington, Oregon, and Arizona were made off-limits to Japanese nationals and Americans of Japanese descent. The last internment camp closed by the Executive Order of President Harry S. Truman on June 26, 1946.

Filipinos started to come to Cleveland after 1950. Koreans didn't come in large groups until the 1970's when US immigration quotas changed. Cambodians and Vietnamese came after 1970 and the Vietnam War. Indians started coming in the early 1960's. But as Ren always pointed out, the Chinese were first.

Chapter 17 – The Present

While Ren was working on history and DJ concentrated on the current situation, Peggy Powell was using her artistic nature to bring the project together. She was a nature buff (Ren affectionately called her a "tree-hugger") and artist who could identify variations of plants from 50 feet away. She didn't have the tech chops of DJ or Ren but she brought a different perspective, and an artist's eye, to their projects.

She was as introverted as Ren was outgoing and often hid her face behind her long locks parted in the middle. Her green eyes popped out from her collection of oversized glasses.

Peggy and Ren's research turned up some interesting items for their documentary. When the first Chinese immigrants arrived was shrouded in mystery but the general belief is that it was in the mid-1800s. There were no official documents and the old books that they found either had just a passing reference or none at all. Most of the information was gleaned from stories passed on from generations. Ren's language skills and Peggy's friendly demeanor worked in combination to extract some of these tales.

As the Chinese population grew there were still the familiar Cantonese and Mandarin dialects but a growing number of restaurants with food from other regions such as Szechuan from Sichuan province and Hunan with the ubiquitous chili peppers, garlic, and shallots.

As with so many cultures, food was key to the family and heritage. An elderly immigrant told Peggy that an age old popular Chinese greeting is "Have you eaten rice yet?" The Thai invitation to a meal translates to "Come and eat rice."

After a half hour of facts like this from their research, DJ confronted Peggy and Ren. "This is interesting but how does it help us prove Henry Fong was innocent?"

Thanks to attorney Margaret Wong, the trio was able to locate Henry Fong's family. "Margaret is incredible," Peggy stated. "I searched all the records I could find and made dozens of calls trying to find Henry Fong with no luck. But she came through – again." It turns out the Fong family had closed their restaurant and moved to Mansfield, Ohio to be close to their incarcerated relative.

Ren couldn't believe his luck. As a film buff he was a big fan of the 1994 classic movie The Shawshank Redemption. It was filmed in Mansfield, Ohio at the Ohio State Reformatory which the world knew as Shawshank State Penitentiary. Mansfield was about 80 miles south of Cleveland, almost halfway to Columbus.

Peggy kept them entertained on the drive with interesting, to her at least, facts about Mansfield that her research had uncovered. "Did you know," she asked, "that this was where they made those scary driver's education films with the gruesome images of fatal automobile accidents?"

"Did you know," she continued "that besides the Shawshank Redemption, the Ohio State Reformatory was featured in scenes of the movies Tango & Cash and Air Force One?"

"Did you know that Johnny Appleseed is considered to be from Mansfield? Luke Perry from Beverly Hills 90210 was born there too!"

And on and on. She continued her non-stop monolog with "Did you know that Mansfield was home of the Isaly Dairy Company which was famous for creating the Klondike Bar?"

Ren had heard enough. He riffed on the familiar question from the commercials "What would you do for a Klondike Bar?" and asked, "Peggy, if I gave you a Klondike Bar would you give it a rest?"

DJ laughed and Peggy slunk back in the seat. "I was just trying to make the trip more interesting" she pouted.

DJ's phone chirped "You have arrived at your destination" and the three pulled into the driveway of a modest bungalow, home to the Fong family.

Chapter 18 – The Present

They had called ahead and were greeted at the door by Jason Fong, nephew of Henry. He had told them that he could prove that his uncle was innocent and was grateful that someone was reopening the case.

Ren said hello to Jason in Cantonese, "néih hóu" and Jason replied with the same. That sounded a lot like the Mandarin hello that DJ was learning, "nǐ hǎo." "I'll never learn it," he sighed to himself.

Ren and the nephew started talking rapidly in Chinese and then they burst into laughter. It's true," Ren laughed in English. "They do all look alike," pointing at DJ and Peggy.

They met a few other members of the Fong family who told how they had heard about the story their whole life and visited

"Uncle Henry" when they could, but didn't have much new information to offer. They marveled at the resemblance between Ren and photos they had seen of their uncle when he was young.

Tea was served and Henry's nephew Jason began his presentation. "My Uncle Henry told me how these guys at the bar would mock him and insult him and then one day they beat him up and stole all his stuff. He said the next thing he knew he was being arrested and it's been a nightmare ever since. He swears he didn't kill that guy or any of the homeless people (he calls them hobos) that were murdered. And I believe him."

DJ and Ren peppered Jason with questions as Peggy stared intently and occasionally doodled something in her notebook. DJ said, "We have to ask. Why did he plead guilty and confess if he didn't do it?" Jason said that he had asked his uncle the same thing and was told the story of the sleazy lawyer threatening the death penalty and all the shame that would be brought upon his family.

Ren was nodding vigorously through the entire explanation and said, "See? See? That makes sense. He didn't do it?"

DJ asked a few more questions about the evidence and Jason suggested that they visit his uncle in prison to hear directly from him. "Sounds good," said DJ "but I have one more question. If your uncle didn't kill that guy and the others, who did?"

"That's the mystery," a suddenly sad looking Jason agreed.

It took another intervention from Margaret Wong to get them clearance to visit Henry Fong in prison. All three were shaken as they entered the gates of the huge prison. It was one thing seeing it in the movies but it was chilling being there in person. In the back of his mind Ren had wondered about shooting one of his films at the prison but quickly decide it was just too dismal. "I feel like we are in Azkaban and the Dementors are about to swoop down on us" he said and the others, all Harry Potter fans, nodded in agreement.

Their IDs were checked and their pockets emptied. They were led down several halls and every time a gate behind them clanged shut, they jumped. Jason noticed and said, "Believe me, you won't get used to it."

Finally they arrived at a dank, drab area with a dozen or so tables and chairs bolted to the floor. After what seemed like hours, another gate opened and two guards assisted an elderly man in a prison orange jumpsuit to their table. Even after all these years and good behavior, Henry was still shackled both hands and feet.

Henry Fong looked broken down and defeated. He had long ago accepted his fate that he was unjustly incarcerated for someone else's crime and all hope was gone.

Ren studied the man's face. It was the striking resemblance to him of that photo in the newspaper that had started all this. He wondered if this is how he would look decades down the road. Jason spoke to his uncle in a mixture of English and Cantonese and the old man nodded. Yes he would tell the story one more time but he had no hope left.

Chapter 19 – The Present

DJ and Peggy had assumed that Ren would lead the questioning but he was too absorbed at looking at the man's face. Henry Fong was staring back at Ren and it suddenly dawned on him that he was looking at a younger version of himself. The tension was palpable and then Henry said in English, "What a good looking guy you are!" and they all laughed with relief.

Henry told his story. He told about the family restaurant and how he dressed like a caricature because it was good for business. He didn't mind he said because people would tip more if he put on a little show. Most places were friendly and they had a good laugh – sometimes at his expense - but he didn't mind. He was going to own the family restaurant one day and buy three more. He had plans! The streets were lined with gold in America – until they weren't.

He told how it was always nerve wracking to get an order from the little bar at 30th and Payne because he never knew what kind of crowd to expect. He liked the Irish fireman and Dana, the owner, and some of the regulars but there was that core group that was just plain no good. They had robbed others in the neighborhood too – like Stanley from the deli.

He told how he felt bad for some of the others like the boys they called Flash and Peanuts Popcorn Bobbie. He especially felt bad for the young mother Dorothy and her almost teenage daughter. They were too pretty, even in their shabby clothes, to be spared ugly comments from Marko, Miro and their cohorts.

Then he told about that night. His voice got quieter as he told about the excitement of the large order and then the brutality that followed. Yes, he wanted to get back at them but would never do anything to bring shame to his family. Even though they shamed him by cutting off his ponytail.

Everyone was silent. Then with a straight face, Henry lightened the mood by telling Ren, "You should grow a ponytail. We look good in them!"

The relief was very welcome and he told the rest of his story about the sleazy lawyer, pleading guilty and the rest.

"Why would I murder a bunch of hobos and try to burn them?" he replied to a question. "I was too busy working in the family business. I never met them and would never kill them. There was no reason!"

"What was I doing after the beating during the time that Marko was killed? I was hobbling home. I couldn't ride my bike so I was trying to get home. I had to walk from 30th and Payne to 21st and Rockwell – and it took me time because of the beating. I was sore."

DJ pressed on. "I'm sorry to be so blunt with these questions but if we are going to help you we need all the facts we can get." Henry waved his hand to indicate that DJ should continue.

"How do you explain your bike being near the scene?" DJ asked. "Someone must have taken it from Dana's alley," he answered. "The tires were slashed and my legs were sore so I couldn't ride it. So I left it there. Somebody must have taken it."

The questions and answers continued. Finally DJ asked his final question. "How do you explain the eye witnesses that saw you near the tracks that night around the time Marko was killed?"

"They must have been lying. I went right home after the beating and was there till the police arrested me," he answered.

"Maybe the eye witnesses were the killers," Ren ventured. "They blamed you to cover their own crime." Henry shook his head. "No, they were all honest people with alibis. Even my crummy lawyer was able to find that out."

They sat in silence for a few minutes and then were shocked as Peggy pushed her glasses up the bridge of her nose and blurted out, "If you didn't kill them, then who did?"

"That's what I've been trying to figure out for decades," Henry replied sadly.

Chapter 20 – The Past

The bar phone rang and Dana, the owner and only bartender on duty, stubbed out his cigarette butt and picked it up. "Bud Sweeney?" he repeated, looking over at the fireman. Sweeney shook his head vigorously and waved his hands. "Nope, he's not here Mrs. Sweeney," lied the bartender. Bud sighed and knew he would have to leave an extra dime tip for his collaborator.

He knew he should be home with the family but he couldn't get the case of Henry Fong out of his mind. He had dealt with Henry and his family and just could not believe that he could be the vicious murderer of the hobos and then Marko. And to try and burn the bodies? It did not seem possible. But Henry confessed – why?

He ordered one last shot of Old Crow and a fishbowl of draft and lit a Pall Mall. At least the bar was quieter since the murder. Miro and the others had stopped coming around.

When he had visited the crime scene he was left with some nagging questions. He couldn't pin it down but his years of experience told him that Marko's murder was different than the others.

The neighborhood seemed surprised that Henry had killed Marko but there were no tears shed for the bully. Some who didn't know the situation were willing to accept the outcome, blaming the "Chinaman" and said "you just can't trust those people."

When Bud stopped into Stanley's Deli for a pound of bologna for the family, the owner told him "I'd like to give Henry a medal." "Yeah, you were pretty mad at them," Bud probed. "Didn't you want to take one of them out yourself?" "I sure thought of it Lieutenant but believe me I would have used my service revolver and shot him in both kneecaps first. And I wouldn't have wasted a match trying to burn the guy."

Bud unofficially spoke with others who were not so blunt but Flash, Peanuts Popcorn Bobbie, Dorothy and Anna Cat and others were all relieved that the bully was dead and his brother and crew gone.

Seamus and other regulars at Dana's were more relaxed and there was often a toast offered to Henry as the night's drinking went on. Seamus, who still seemed remarkably flush with cash, usually led the tribute. Everyone seemed happy, Bud thought, except Henry who would be in prison for life and his poor family who were shutting down the restaurant and moving away.

Bud just could not believe that Henry had not only killed Marko but all of those hobos as well. It didn't make sense. He couldn't stop reflecting on his firemen's instincts that told him Marko's murder was different from the other Chinatown murders. But there was nothing he could do. He finished his drinks, paid his tab, left Dana a tip and headed up Payne two blocks to the family house.

Chapter 21 – The Present

The three were more convinced than ever that Henry was innocent and the drive home from Mansfield was unusually somber. Instead of stopping for food they decided to visit the area where the murders took place. They didn't expect to unearth any clues after so many decades but thought it might give them some perspective. And frankly they were running out of ideas.

They were all very familiar with the area around East 30th and Payne. It was now the center of Cleveland's AsiaTown and looked nothing like it used to.

But they were concerned with the Chinatown in Cleveland that was still centered around East 21st and Rockwell. Originally, Chinatown was just the Shanghai Restaurant, the Three Sisters, the Golden Coins and the Ming Tsang Grocery Store. Since Henry's family's restaurant was located there that's where they began. They parked across from Sichuan Hot Pot Cuisine at 2162 Rockwell and Emperor's Palace next door at 2136.

Peggy loved the area because of the dozen stone statues of Chinese Zodiac animals that lined the street. The Zhong Shan Merchants erected them and they were popular photo spots long before social media.

Both Ren and DJ had attended an event a few years ago at Emperor's Palace with community leaders including Margaret Wong, Anthony Yen and others. Zhongshan, China is a sister city of Cleveland, Ohio and a delegation from there presented the city with a gift - a bronze statue of Dr. Sun Yat-sen, the first president and founding father of the Republic of China.

Considered the father of modern China, Sun Yat-sen was from Zhongshan. Zhongshan is a growing metropolis of over 4.4 million people in the southern, Cantonese-speaking region of China, the historic source of Northeast Ohio's Chinese community. He visited Cleveland and Oberlin College during his exile years in the United States and spoke in 1911 at the Old Stone Church, where a plaque commemorates the moment.

Old Stone Church, located on the northwest corner of Public Square in Cleveland, wanted to both help the immigrants and convert them by providing Chinese language church services. Two notable members of the congregation, Mary and Marian Trapp, founded a Chinese Sunday School. It was a natural spot for Sun Yat-sen to speak.

Besides the monumental visit from Sun Yat-sen, Cleveland Chinatown was home to local Tong Wars. Originally, Chinese immigrants worked in the gold mines of California and moved on to the Transcontinental Railroad. They moved east as racial discrimination grew and found work in laundries and restaurants. The Chinese formed merchant associations known as tongs, to protect their businesses. The tongs were a combination of labor guild and gang so naturally feuds developed among them. In 1925 the feuds became known as the Tong Wars.

The two main tongs that grew in Cleveland were the Hip Sing Tong and the On Leong Tong. The On Leong tong had purchased land along Rockwell Avenue. Some say that was the start of the Tong Wars. Businesses were leaving Ontario Street downtown and moving to Rockwell where the On Leong tong had their headquarters. This was the start of Cleveland's Chinatown. And where Henry Fong and his family built their restaurant.

They visited all the establishments that were open and Ren led the conversations in Cantonese. As expected, they didn't find anyone who was alive at the time and remembered the story. One octogenarian told Ren that she had heard of Henry Fong and the case but didn't know anything.

How do you find evidence from a crime decades ago? St. Columbkille's Church and School were razed in 1957 for construction of the Inner Belt Freeway (Interstate 90). Chin's was long gone. Stanley's Delicatessen had closed and been replaced by the massive Dave's Supermarket on Payne only to eventually move out of the neighborhood itself.

They drove to the spot of the murders. The area by the railroad tracks near East 26th street and Lakeside was still pretty much undeveloped and abandoned. The train tracks were still there and the three researchers were more convinced than ever that someone could have hopped on and off the trains there and murdered people in what was then the hobo village. But that didn't explain the eyewitnesses who saw Henry Fong there. But it did give Ren an idea.

Chapter 22 – The Present

They were starting to get hungry so they drove a few blocks to 31st and St Clair for Slyman's corned beef. Slyman's was nationally known as "home of the biggest and best corned beef." President George W. Bush had eaten at Slyman's as did LeBron James, Rachael Ray, the Bare Naked Ladies, Michael Symon and many others.

They all ordered the traditional CB – corned beef on rye with mustard and a dill pickle – and grabbed a table. The sandwiches were huge and DJ and Ren were eager to tease on-again-off-again vegan Peggy if she didn't eat much. But she surprised them – and herself – by chowing down on more than either of the guys!

They all had doggie bags for the leftovers but Peggy had reason to brag. That is until they got back in the car and she let out an earth-shattering burp that shocked them into silence before they exploded in laughter. She was beet red but laughing as hard as the others and when she snorted, they all lost it again.

They knew their work was done for the day. Nobody could concentrate after that.

After visiting the tracks where the murders took place Ren had an idea. He was reluctant to go back to the microfiche machines and look at old newspapers but he knew it was important. If Henry was indeed the killer, than the murders in Chinatown would have stopped when he was arrested. If they continued in the same fashion, Henry would be cleared!

He loaded up issues of the three Cleveland newspapers and started reading headlines for a few days and then weeks after the murder. He really wanted to find something about a body being found, smoldering, near the tracks off of Lakeside. Unfortunately he found none.

He did find an article from a few months later from a lawyer named Jack Johnson who was running for mayor. The candidate had referenced the "Chinatown Murders" and how he had put a stop to them by convincing his client to confess. "What a sleaze!" Ren thought. "Weren't defense lawyers supposed to defend their client no matter what?" Henry's own lawyer was using his wrongful conviction to further his own career. Ren quickly scrolled to the November papers and was happy and relieved to see that Jack Johnson was trounced in the mayoral election.

"But that doesn't help Henry," he said, slurping on a honeydew smoothie from Koko's Bakery. He had just recounted his activities to DJ and Peggy over a much needed snack.

DJ had a Vietnamese iced coffee and Peggy had something green resembling her trademark "Peggy." They drank silently until DJ looked up and said, "Ren, that was a great idea. It's just a little off!"

Ren looked puzzled but his lips never left the straw. DJ said, "The Cleveland newspapers wouldn't report the absence of a crime, would they? So it's not surprising that you didn't find anything like that." Ren and Peggy looked puzzled.

DJ continued, "Newspapers only report crimes when they happen so if no similar crimes were committed the Cleveland newspapers would have nothing to report so you wouldn't find anything."

"Are you sure that's just iced coffee in that glass, Deej?" Ren asked.

DJ ignored the comment and continued. "But a newspaper in a city where a crime was committed would publish it, right? So if you find reports of similar murders taking place in a city along the railroad tracks, that would mean that the real killer had moved on."

"And that Henry Fong is innocent!" Peggy blurted.

Chapter 23 – The Present

Ren went back to the library the next day and retrieved microfiche of stories fitting the time frame from Erie, PA and Toledo newspapers. Nothing. He was tired and ready to give up but he knew that Henry was innocent and wanted to make sure that he did everything he could to prove it.

So Ren expanded his search to the Detroit and Pittsburgh papers. He finally found a story in the Detroit Free Press archives that was a possibility. A man who rode the rails, the paper identified him as a hobo, was notorious for drinking and gambling too much with his peers.

The story told how he had lost a card game, and all his money, to a fellow drifter and knocked him unconscious with a board. Thinking him dead, he grabbed back all the money and then grabbed a burning stick from the campfire. He approached the supine man but the others intervened. Waking up and seeing what his attacker had done, the vagrant pulled out a small pistol and shot and killed his assailant. Later his claim of self-defense was upheld and he was ordered to leave Detroit and never come back.

Just to be safe, Ren checked later dates of the archives and there were no more such killings reported. He was more convinced than ever that Henry had not been the Chinatown Murderer but he knew such circumstantial evidence would not be enough to free him. They had to identify Marko's murderer in order to free Henry.

They knew the answer but just in case they called Margaret Wong with the new "evidence" and she confirmed that it was not sufficient to overturn the conviction.

They were running out of ideas. One other site they needed to visit was Dana's at East 30th and Payne where Henry had been beaten and robbed by Marko, Miro and their crew. Their expectations were not high because Dana's at East 30th and Payne was long gone.

What had been the popular neighborhood bar was now the heart of Cleveland's AsiaTown, centered at the Asia Plaza building on the corner. Asia Plaza was created by lifelong

Clevelander John Louie in 1988. He and Tak Wai Ko saw the growth in the Chinese and broader Asian communities in the neighborhood and thought they could support an Asian Market. So John moved his existing store, Hall One, to this location.

But it was Donna and Willie Hom who were most responsible for Asia Plaza and AsiaTown. Donna was born in Guangdong province in southern China. She married her husband Willie Hom in 1960 and emigrated to the U.S. settling in Youngstown, Ohio.

After arriving in the U.S., she had four sons and saw the need to earn more money to support her family. In the 1960s, she worked as a waitress at her mother-in-law's Chinese restaurant (called Ding Ho) in Youngstown and at Perkins Pancake House in Austintown. As the economy in Youngstown deteriorated in the late 1960s, Willie and she realized that the family would need to move to a larger city in order to economically survive.

In 1970, they moved the family to Fairview Park, a suburb of Cleveland. She worked at two west side Chinese restaurants as a waitress. Then in 1973, the Homs opened their first Chinese restaurant, King Wah, in Rocky River across from Westgate Mall. The location was originally a biker bar but they turned it into a Chinese restaurant after extensive remodeling. As the business grew, they expanded the restaurant to accommodate more patrons.

They bought the building housing King Wah in 1977. In 1979, they bought an east side Chinese restaurant (located at LaPlace Mall in Beachwood) called Ho Ho and renamed it Ho Wah. The east side restaurant was an immediate success.

By the 1980s, the taste of American customers for Chinese food began to change. Customers were becoming tired of Cantonese-style/Americanized Chinese food (for example, egg foo young or chicken chow mein) so Donna began to include Chinese dishes in the menus from other parts of China. People loved the Szechwan, Mandarin and Hunan dishes like Kung Pao chicken.

There had been much talk in the mid-1980s by Chinese-Americans in Cleveland who dreamed of building a Chinatown on Payne Avenue and Superior Avenue that would be comparable to ones in Toronto and New York City and that would attract Asian investment to Northeast Ohio. In 1988, Willie and Donna decided to get involved in the development of a Cleveland Chinatown.

They purchased an old warehouse where Dana's had once stood, at the northwest corner of Payne Avenue and East 30th Street. They began to develop Asia Plaza Mall under the supervision of their son, Stephen. In May 1991, they opened Li Wah Restaurant at Asia Plaza.

Li Wah was designed for Asian customers by serving authentic Chinese dishes and dim sum. Dim sum consists of a large range of small Chinese dishes that are traditionally offered by servers pushing a cart of the food throughout the restaurant. Patrons point to what they want and the carts continue their rounds. Li Wah became known for their delicious dim sum offerings and the Sunday dim sum brunch is always packed with Asians and non-Asians alike.

Soon, many small shops also opened at Asia Plaza. Sadly, Willie passed away in September 1991 but Donna and her family continued the dream.

In 2004, Donna purchased the old Cleveland Food Bank building, connected it to Asia Plaza Mall, and remodeled the building under Stephen's supervision. Most of the Cleveland Food Bank building was rented to an Asian grocery store.

Donna's dream was to create a vibrant Asian community in the East 30th Street and Payne Avenue area. Her dream has become a reality as dozens of new Asian businesses have been established from East 30th to East 55th Street on Superior Avenue and Payne Avenue. While the area at East 21st and

Rockwell is still called Chinatown, the growing area centered at 30th and Payne was named AsiaTown.

In 2010, Donna opened up Asia Plaza Mall for the first annual Cleveland Asian Festival, which now attracts 50,000 visitors, Asian cultural performance acts and community resources each year. Dozens of restaurants and food trucks serve food that ranges from Himalayan to Filipino to Indian to Korean and so on – and of course Chinese.

The complex is now actively managed by Steve Hom. Ren was good friends with the Hom family so he led the three into Li Wah. As expected, Steve had no recollection of the bar that had been there decades ago or the people that might have frequented it.

The trip wasn't a total waste as Ren pointed to the Har Gao (shrimp dumplings) and Sesame Balls from the passing dim sum cart. DJ opted for Sticky Rice Lotus Leaf and Sui Mei (pork and shrimp dumpling). Peggy was still a little green from her huge meal at Slyman's so she declined food and just sipped tea. Ren nudged DJ and pointed to the Chicken Feet on the dim sum cart and surreptitiously pointing his chopstick at Peggy. DJ stifled a laugh and shook his head "no" realizing that just looking at the chicken feet would send Peggy to the restroom.

They finished the small plates and then looked at each other sadly. "It looks like we are at a dead end," Ren admitted.

Their mood lifted as they heard the familiar pounding of a drum in the Plaza. It was the grand opening of another store in Asia Plaza and it was being celebrated with a Lion Dance for good fortune. The lion dance is usually performed during Chinese New Year and other traditional, cultural and religious festivals. But it is also often performed at important occasions such as this business opening event believed to bring good luck and fortune.

In the Chinese Lion Dance there are usually two performers who wear a lion costume and mimic a lion's movements to bring good luck and fortune. One controls the head and the other manipulates the tail end. They dance to a steady drum beat often accompanied by gongs and cymbals.

Ren had to stop himself from correcting a tourist who was explaining the "Dragon Dance" to his companions. The Dragon Dance is performed by many people who hold the long body of the dragon on poles while the Lion Dance is usually just the two people.

In Cleveland the Lion Dance is synonymous with the Kwan Family. When he was fourteen George Kwan Jr. and his brothers were learning Chinese kung fu. His father, George Kwan Sr., wanted the boys to learn lion dancing. They practiced under several teachers and ended up performing with the On Leong Merchants Association Lion Dance Team.

They learned more about lion dancing and usually practiced at night under the street lights on the sidewalk on Rockwell Avenue in Chinatown or in front of the Hip Sing Association building on Payne Ave. For several years they continued their intense training and eventually George Sr. declared it was time to form their own team. The Kwan Family Lion Dance Team was formed in 1987 and has been performing ever since for thousands of people in hundreds of venues across Ohio.

Ren pointed out that the Kwan Family's lions are the traditional Southern lion originating from the Guangzhou area of China. He said that George Jr. told him that they are incredibly expensive and that fortunately they had a benefactor for their first lion.

"Can you guess who it was?" Ren asked. "Margaret!" both DJ and Peggy answered at the same time. "Nope," Ren chuckled. "Close but no cigar. It was George Hwang, a good friend of George Kwan Sr. who also owned the Pearl of the Orient restaurant in Rocky River. Oh yeah… he's Margaret's brother!"

"What a family," Peggy mused as Ren went on about the need for lots of repairs and reconditioning of the lions each year – especially during Chinese New Year when the team performs about forty shows in a month.

The drumming intensified and the lion approached. The store owner had hung the customary green lettuce from the top of his storefront for the traditional custom of "cai qing" which means "plucking the greens". The lettuce (greens or qing) are tied together with a red envelope containing money. In Chinese, cǎi (pluck) also sounds like cái which translate to "fortune."

The lion dances to the drumbeat and climbs to investigate the greens. He will eat the greens and then spit out the "chewed" lettuce to the delight of the audience. Of course he will keep the red envelope, which is the pay for the team. The ceremony often includes lucky fruits like oranges which the lion tosses to the crowd with his mouth.

Ren was able to snatch a flying orange from the lion but reluctantly handed it over to a young girl who had been watching longingly. "Oh well", he said, "back to work."

Chapter 24 – The Present

They decided they needed to get Margaret Wong's advice yet again. They hated to bother her but they were desperate. They drove to 32nd and Chester but Margaret was in her New York office that day so they called her. Her assistant said she was just finishing her radio show and asked them to hold.

After a few minutes, Margaret came on the line and congratulated the trio on their efforts but cautioned that after all this time they would most likely need a confession from the real killer to overturn Henry Fong's conviction.

"Have you spoken to every single person connected to the case?" she asked.

"The ones we could locate." Ren responded. "It happened decades ago so people have moved or died or forgotten."

"I may have someone for you to talk with," she replied. "I have another meeting now but check your e-mail later today." And she hung up.

The next few hours were excruciating. The three were gathered in their makeshift office staring at the PC monitor while Ren hit "Refresh" and "Get New Mail" every few seconds. "You're going to wear out the F5 key Ren," Peggy complained but she and DJ were just as eager.

Every time a new batch of messages was displayed in the company inbox they got excited. Of course, most was spam or stupid jokes. Nothing from Margaret.

It was now after 5PM and they would have given up but knowing Margaret's demanding schedule they knew that her message might not come for many more hours. "How about some Mexican?" Ren asked. Peggy complained that Ren was always hungry and always eating but still never gained a pound. It wasn't fair.

As they scanned the taco menu a new batch of messages appeared. Including one from Margaret Wong! The message was short: "Contact Dr. Samuel Norton. Tell him I sent you." It included a phone number.

DJ and Ren wanted to call right away but Peggy convinced them to wait till the morning. None of them slept well that night wondering who the heck Dr. Samuel Norton was.

At 8:59 AM the next day Ren had pressed 6 of the 7 numbers into his phone. As soon as it turned 9 AM he hit the 7th number. Listening on the speakerphone, they all seemed surprised when an individual answered. They had expected a doctor's office.

"How may I help you?" an older voice asked. "Can we speak to Dr. Norton please?" DJ asked. "That's me," he responded.

DJ explained that Margaret Wong had advised them to contact him. "Yes, I was expecting your call. Margaret gave me a head up yesterday. Isn't she the best?" he asked.

They agreed and asked if they could come and see him. He agreed but said, "Let's have lunch at P.J. McIntyre's Irish Pub. I haven't been there in ages." They agreed and he added, "Oh yes, I will need a ride."

They were surprised but agreed and Dr. Norton gave an address on the near west side of Cleveland. Ren searched it and saw that it was an assisted living facility. "That must be where he works," Peggy surmised.

They pulled up in front of the place a little before noon and Ren hopped in the back seat with Peggy while DJ went inside to get the Doctor. It was a nice place and as DJ waited he wondered what kind of doctor Dr. Norton was.

Chapter 25 – The Present

In a few minutes an elderly man with a shock of white hair ambled out with the aid of a nurse and a walker. His one foot dragged but he maneuvered pretty well. DJ and the doctor shook hands and the nurse said, "Now you behave yourself Doc."

The doctor grinned ear to ear and headed for the door with DJ. DJ opened the front seat door and held the walker as the man finessed his way into the seat. DJ folded up the walker, pressed his car key to open the trunk and placed it in there.

Doctor Norton greeted the backseat passengers and DJ pulled out. "So Doctor…" DJ asked but the Doctor said, "Not Yet. Wait till we get to P.J. McIntyre's. I haven't had a real Irish breakfast in years so let's talk after we eat."

DJ drove to the pub on Lorain in the Kamm's Corners neighborhood of Cleveland. The neighborhood has the highest concentration of Irish Americans in Cleveland and Cuyahoga County.

Kamm's Corners was named for a local merchant, Oswald Kamm, who had emigrated from Switzerland to Cleveland. In 1875 he purchased four acres at the southwest corner of Lorain Avenue and Rocky River Drive and opened a general store which also served as the local post office. The original store was torn down in 1900 and a second store was built on the same site which still stands in the Kamm's Corners retail district.

There is a landmark Kamm's Corners clock at the intersection of Lorain Avenue and Rocky River Drive. P.J. McIntyre's is right across the street.

DJ parked and then helped the doctor with his walker and they entered what seemed like a slice of Ireland. It was the most authentic Irish pub that any of the three had ever seen.

They found a table and Dr. Norton shooed away the menu that the waitress offered. "I'll have the Irish breakfast," he said. The three looked at each other well aware that it was now after noon.

"Don't look that way," the doctor scolded. "They are famous for their Irish breakfast and it's served all day." Peggy ordered a California Turkey Wrap but Ren and DJ decided to try the Irish breakfast. When in Rome…

"Is this really what the Irish have for breakfast?" Ren asked as their huge plates arrived. "I don't know," the doctor responded "but it sure is delicious. There's my old friend Gerry. I'll ask him."

Dr. Norton waved at a man sitting a few tables away and motioned him to come over. Gerry Quinn walked over and slapped his old friend on the back. "I haven't seen you in ages, Doc," Quinn remarked with a brogue. Gerry Quinn had come to the US from his native Garracloon in County Mayo in Ireland decades ago but he still had the lilt of an Irish brogue. His popular weekly Irish Radio Show had been on the air since 1980 and had won numerous awards. Who better to explain their Irish breakfast plates?

Gerry told them that the breakfast is often called a "fry" in Ireland and explained that the plates had beans, bangers, mushrooms, eggs, hash browns, rashers, tomato, soda bread, black pudding and white pudding. And of course a cup of tea.

Seeing their still puzzled expressions, he continued. "Rashers are thin slices of back bacon and side bacon that look more like ham than what we know as bacon in the US. Bangers are just sausages."

The Doctor and guys chowed down on the feast as Peggy picked at her wrap. "This is really good," Ren commented with his mouth full. What's this?" He pointed at the black pudding. When Gerry explained that it was blood sausage and that the white pudding was similar but without the blood, Peggy put down her fork and hurried off to the restroom. DJ and Ren howled with laughter.

Peggy returned a few minutes later and it was obvious that she was trying to control herself. She spoke very businesslike and asked Dr. Samuel to tell how he knew Margaret. She was trying so hard and so serious that the guys burst out in laughter again before regaining their composure and apologizing.

The waitress came back and took the three completely clean breakfast plates and asked Peggy if she wanted a box for her barely eaten food. Peggy shook her head "no" and they guys almost bit their tongues trying not to laugh.

"I'm going to tell your story of the black pudding on my radio show next week Peggy if that's alright with you," Quinn asked with a twinkle in his eyes. Peggy just nodded and Gerry said his goodbyes and went back to his table.

"Okay Doc," Ren asked. "Why did Margaret want us to talk with you?" Dr. Samuel Norton explained that he was a retired orthopedic doctor who had treated Margaret's sister Cecilia years ago after a skiing accident. The families became friends and they shared stories over many dinners over the years. "Margaret remembered a story I had once told about a murder in Chinatown when I was a kid. She said you were investigating it."

The trio looked at each other and DJ asked eagerly, "What do you know about the murders?"

The Doctor wiped his mouth, took a sip of tea and replied, "I was there."

Chapter 26 – The Present

Ren almost spit out his tea. "You were there?" he exclaimed. How? Why...?"

"Well, I wasn't there for the actual murder but I knew some of the people involved. I was just a kid and had a condition called Spinal Stenosis where the spaces within the bones in my spine got narrow. That put pressure on the nerves in the area and caused all kinds of problems like pain, tingling, numbness and weakness in my legs. It also caused me to have trouble with balance."

"Sorry to hear that Doc," DJ responded impatiently. "But what does that have to do with the murders?" "I'm getting to that young man," Dr. Norton countered. "My leg condition caused a notable limp and some of the mean people would mock me. One even started calling me "Flash" instead of Sammy. The Flash was a comic book hero first introduced in 1939. He had super speed so calling me Flash was intentionally hurtful."

"Oh we know about the Flash," Ren said. "He's one of my favorite DC Comics superheroes. Why I remember in one Justice League of America comic that…"

"Ren!" Peggy blurted. "We can talk about comics later. Doctor please go on. That was so cruel for them to call you that."

"Yes it was my dear," he replied. "But it inspired me to study the disease and led me to my long career in Orthopedics. That's the story I originally shared with Margaret. But I can see how anxious you three are so I'll get back to the story. By coincidence or karma, the first person to call me Flash was a victim of what they called the Chinatown Murders, a devil named Marko Pavlovic."

"Please, tell us everything you can remember," Peggy pleaded. Dr. Norton told about Marko and his brother Miro and some of the other thugs. "They didn't just pick on me," he continued." They went after anyone weaker or different. There was a gentle soul named Bobbie that they were always abusing and they gave him a demeaning nickname as well. They went after a woman and her young daughter who sold groceries in the neighborhood tavern. They particularly went after immigrants – anyone who looked different – but especially one young man."

And he paused and stared at Ren. "You!" he pointed at Ren. "You look exactly like the poor soul they targeted."

"I hear he was really good looking," Ren joked and proceeded to tell the background of their investigation.

"Ah, I see," said the Doctor when Ren was finished. "I can tell you one thing. Henry Fong did not kill Marko Pavlovic and certainly was not involved in the other Chinatown murders. He was a kind soul and always treated me well. I was always surprised that he confessed to the crime."

"That's all well and good, Doc, and we agree, but do you have any evidence or other memories that could help us clear Henry?" DJ asked.

"I wish I did," the doctor said dejectedly. "But I wasn't there that night and didn't see anything. If you see Henry again, tell him I'm sorry."

They got back into the car and drove in silence back to the nursing home. DJ opened the trunk, got the walker and helped Doctor Norton to the door. Ren and Peggy said goodbye but stayed in the car, too depressed.

"How was your lunch Doctor," a nurse asked as they entered? "Looking good Sammy," a resident chimed in as they passed the common area. "Good afternoon Samuel" a prim and proper resident wearing pearls and a hat greeted. DJ couldn't wait to get out of there. It seemed like there were a lot of lonely people there eager to see someone new and be a part of something different. "Did you bring me anything Flash?" a woman asked. "Sam, my man," said another. It continued until they got to Dr. Norton's room where DJ thanked the man for his help and promised they would visit again.

DJ hurried to the car, jumped in and sped off. He just wanted to get away from there as soon as possible. Each of the three was lost in their own thoughts. DJ kept thinking about the sad people in that common area.

Then it hit him. "We have to go back!" he cried and did an illegal U-turn on West 25th.

Chapter 27 – The Present

The sudden U-turn sent Ren sprawling onto Peggy. "What are you doing Deej!" he shrieked. "It's a longshot but something just struck me," DJ answered. He explained that everyone in the facility had greeted the man as Doctor Norton or Sammy or Sam or even Samuel. But one elderly woman had called him Flash. "Only people from that era and neighborhood knew him as Flash. Maybe she knows something else?"

"I guess it's worth a shot," Peggy replied, smoothing out her oversized handbag that Ren had landed on.

This time all three entered the facility and DJ went up to the desk. Ren and Peggy hung back by the entrance. A different nurse was on duty and asked if she could help them. "Can we speak with Dr. Norton please?" DJ asked.

"I'm sorry but he just started his nap and we don't want to wake him. He had a big day I hear."

DJ explained that he was with him that afternoon and asked if he could look into the common area. He wanted to see if the woman who had called the Doctor "Flash" was there.

"I'm sorry, sir," the nurse replied. "Our privacy rules only allow family and friends of residents to go beyond this point. You can come back tomorrow and see Dr. Norton if you want."

DJ thanked her and headed toward the door with his head hanging down dejectedly. He jerked his head up when he saw Peggy grab Ren's hand and lead him to a Visitor's sign-in book outside the common room. "Come on dear," she urged. "I promised to introduce you to Grandma before the wedding."

This time it was Ren who turned beet red and he shuffled along with Peggy to the common room. They scanned the room and found two elderly women and three men. One woman, dressed as if she was going out on the town, was knitting and the other was rocking back and forth humming to herself. They looked about the same advanced age so Peggy, with Ren in tow, approached the well-dressed woman and asked if she knew Dr. Norton. "Of course I know Samuel," she replied. "He is one of my admirers. I have many, you know."

Peggy thanked her and dragged Ren along with her to the other woman. "Hello," she said. Do you know Dr. Norton?" The woman had a glazed expression and didn't reply right away.

Peggy leaned over and asked again more loudly. After a moment the woman looked up and said, "Honey, I have so many doctors that I can't keep track of all their names."

Peggy tried the various versions of the name – Sam, Samuel, Sammy, etc. – all with the same blank expression and nodding of the head "no." Then Peggy tried the one name she was hoping to be recognized. "Do you know someone named 'Flash'?"

No response. She repeated the question and Ren freed his hand and whispered, "Let's get out of here. This place gives me the creeps."

Peggy was not ready to give up. She held the woman's hand, looked squarely in her eyes and asked again. "Do you know someone named 'Flash'?"

After a few second, the woman's eyes focused and she said, "Of course I know Flash. We live in the same neighborhood. Poor kid has a bad limp."

Peggy and Ren looked at each other excitedly and Peggy asked "Ma'am, what is your name?"

"My name? Why Dot, of course."

Chapter 28 – The Present

An orderly came by and told them visiting hours were over and that they had to prepare the residents for dinner. They asked the woman, now known as Dot, if they could come visit her tomorrow. "Let me check my busy calendar," she quipped before nodding yes.

The two left the facility and DJ was almost bursting to hear what had happened. "I think I got engaged!" Ren responded with a grin. They hopped in the car and Peggy filled him in. "You really are part of the Mod Squad, Peggy," DJ complimented. "That was quick thinking."

DJ and Ren were still full from their Irish breakfast and Peggy was still unable to think about food so they headed to the office for a while before heading home. "We are running out of possibilities," DJ said "so let's hope we get some good info from Dot tomorrow." Ren and Peggy looked at each other and Ren said, "Uh Deej, don't get your hopes up. We spoke with her and she didn't seem all there." And Peggy nodded with a forlorn smile.

The next day they arrived at the facility and Peggy signed in. Luckily, Dot was in the common room, rocking back and forth slowly. They didn't know her last name so it would have been a problem if they had to ask a nurse for her room number. They had stopped for some flowers on the way and Peggy presented them to the woman whose eyes widened with delight. "These are just like the flowers that my Stanley gives me," she said. "Is he with you?"

The three didn't know what to say but Peggy reminded her that they had met yesterday and were visiting today to have a chat. Dot didn't remember the visit from the day before but was happy to have company and even happier to see the look of envy in the woman wearing pearls face as she smelled the flowers.

The three had agreed to go very slowly with their questions and to have Peggy take the lead as much as possible. Ren's boundless energy and DJ's sheer size made them seem intimidating.

Peggy started with some general questions about how she was feeling, did she like the facility, what was her favorite food and so on. It usually took two or three repetitions to get any response and then it was short and guarded. There was a glimmer of recognition when Peggy asked Dot about her family. "Oh my Angel," she sighed. But that was all.

Peggy reminded her about their discussion about "Flash" yesterday but what met with blank stares. Similarly there was no response when she asked about the old neighborhood. Peggy didn't even try to ask about the Chinatown murders.

After another 15 minutes of this the three looked at each other and Peggy told the woman, "Thanks so much for talking with us Dot. We appreciate it. We'll come back another day with more flowers if you like."

The woman nodded and sniffed at the flowers again. An orderly took them to put them in water for her and wheeled her back to her room.

"Well, we tried." Ren sighed as the three signed out and headed for the door. As they opened the door a voice came from behind, "Maybe I can help."

Chapter 29 – The Present

It was Dr. Norton aka Sammy aka Flash. He was sitting in a wheelchair this time, not using his walker like the day before. He saw them looking and said, "Some days are better than others for my legs."

"I should have told you about Dorothy, or Dot as she calls herself, before but as you found out her mind has been unsettled for decades. I didn't think she would be of any help."

Dr. Norton went on to explain that Dot's full name was Dorothy Tomcho and that she, and her daughter Anna Cat, were also victims of Marko, Miro and the other scoundrels in their old neighborhood.

"I had seen Dorothy around the neighborhood and she was a normal kid. She used to hang around Stanley's Deli as a young teen and stack cans and wash fruit until Stanley eventually gave her a part-time job."

"She was mature for her age, if you know what I mean," he continued. "Physically, not socially or mentally. I think she lived with her aunt on 43rd and Superior but we never saw her with any family. She didn't go to St. Columbkille's or the public school on Waring. When she disappeared for months we assumed she had moved away. One day she showed up at Stanley's pushing a stroller and introducing her daughter Anna Catherine. I think it was Stanley who first called the baby Anna Cat and the name stuck – except to Dorothy who always called her Annie."

"You kids have to remember," he went on, "this was decades ago and unwed pregnancies were scandalous. And she was just a young teenager. Nobody knew who Anna Cat's father was and Dorothy was shunned by many in the neighborhood."

The trio were listening intently and reflecting on how hard it must have been for the young girl and her baby. "Is that what made her, uh, like she is?" Ren asked. "Ren!" Peggy reprimanded and glared at him.

"We were all wondering Peggy. I just asked," said Ren. "No, Dorothy was actually very sharp back then," Dr. Norton countered. "She was unable to get a decent job because of the baby. Between the scandal of the young teen mother and her needing to take care of Anna Cat, no companies would hire her.

112

So she figured out a way to take care of the baby and make some money."

He told the trio that Dorothy had gone to Stanley and convinced him to give her groceries on credit and a discount and then she would take them to shops and houses and sell them at full price. She would make her rounds with Anna Cat and keep the funds left over after paying Stanley.

"There was always talk about Stanley being Anna Cat's father but he was an upstanding member of the community and almost three times her age," he added. "For whatever reason he was always helpful to Dorothy and Anna Cat and the arrangement, though hard work, kept them out of the poorhouse."

DJ jumped in and asked, "What were her dealings with Marko Pavlovic? Do you think she can remember anything that might help us clear Henry?"

"Let me answer your second question first," the doctor replied. "When I first moved to this facility a few years ago I made an effort to meet as many of my new neighbors as possible. Dot seemed somewhat familiar to me but I've had so many patients over the years that I certainly can't remember them all."

"She never had visitors but was not anti-social. She spent much of her time in the common area. Sometimes she seemed coherent, other times she rocked and mumbled to herself. I learned from one of the longtime nurses that while she had some symptoms of dementia she had been admitted decades ago for symptoms of neurological trauma. She wasn't "crazy" but she couldn't live on her own."

"When I eventually learned that her name was Dorothy Tomcho it was evident to me that the familiar face was the young mother I knew from 30th and Payne. I tried talking to her about the old days, calling her Dorothy and so on. Most of the time there was no response but sometimes there was recognition in her eyes. When I explained to her that she might remember me as "Flash" her eyes lit up."

Dr. Norton continued with how he gradually got her to talk a little about the old days but if he asked about or even mentioned her daughter Anna Cat she shut down.

"So to finally answer your question young man," he said. "If you talk to her on a good day and at a good time for her you might get some responses but I don't think she will be able to help you with solving the murder."

Chapter 30 – The Present

"Speaking of good and bad days," Dr. Sammy Norton continued," I have had enough for today. I need some rest."

"But what about Dorothy and Marko and the others?" DJ asked. "Not today young man, not today," the doctor replied. He said his goodbyes and wheeled back to his room.

With their heads full of this information, the three trudged back to the car. "It's an interesting and sad story," Peggy said "but I don't see how it helps clear Henry." That's because our brains need some food!" the ever-hungry Ren chimed in. "Let's go eat!"

They drove down West 25th and crossed the Detroit-Superior Bridge. Locals still called it the Detroit-Superior bridge but in 1989 the bridge was renamed the Veterans Memorial Bridge. The bridge is over 3100 feet long and connects Cleveland's near west side over the Cuyahoga River to the east side and Public Square.

The bridge had an interesting history. Construction started in 1914 and ended in 1917. At the time of its completion, the bridge was the largest steel and concrete reinforced bridge in the world.

It was built with a lower level for underground streetcar stations for trams. The Detroit–Superior subway was an underground transit system that operated between 1917 until its closure January 24, 1954. In November 1955, ramps to the lower level were closed.

To DJ, Ren and Peggy – especially Ren – the bridge was cool because of the movie scenes that were shot on it. For example, The Avengers were filmed there in 2012 and Captain America: The Winter Soldier in 2014.

The latest was the 2025 Superman movie filmed in the summer of 2024. Sure, traffic was rerouted for a week or so but all three thought it was worth it to see superheroes and Cleveland landmarks on the big screen.

They arrived at East 38th and St Clair at another favorite AsiaTown restaurant called Bo Loong. Ren liked the Mu Shu pork. Peggy had studied the osmanthus tree and told Ren that his dish was originally spelled moo shi. "It's a dish from northern China, originating from Shandong. It always contains egg and the yellow color is reminiscent of blossoms of the osmanthus tree, after which the dish is named."

Sometimes Ren and DJ were amazed at what Peggy knew. DJ said, "I'm just getting beef with broccoli. Did you know that broccoli is an edible green plant in the cabbage family, Ren?" Ren snorted and DJ apologized to Peggy. "Sorry, I was just teasing. I'm always surprised at what you know." Peggy ordered Braised Tofu with Mushrooms and Pea Pods but didn't dare tell about its etymology.

As they ate, the three went over everything they had learned and what they still needed to find out to clear Henry. "It makes sense why Henry confessed even though he was innocent," Ren stated. "The problem is the credible eyewitnesses. Without an explanation for that we won't be able to clear him."

"Maybe Dorothy/Dot saw something," Peggy ventured.

"And if we can get her to remember and tell us," DJ added. "If not I think we are out of ideas."

Chapter 31 – The Present

Over the next week they called Dr. Norton every day to check on Dorothy's condition. He said he would let them know if she was having a lucid day. So far, no luck.

Then one day his number popped up on their office phone's caller ID and all 3 scrambled to answer it. DJ got their first and answered breathlessly. "Hi kids (they were still 'kids' to the elderly doctor)," the doctor said. "Dot is having a pretty good day. When I told her the flowers still looked pretty she called me Flash and said they were a gift from Stanley. This would be a good time to try and talk with her if you are available."

They rushed to the car and headed for the facility hoping that Dorothy would stay clear headed and have some helpful information.

Dr. Norton was sitting with Dorothy in the common area as the three rushed in. As they approached, Sam motioned for them to calm down and they joined them at the table littered with pieces from several in progress jigsaw puzzles.

"Hi kids," he said, "Did you know that Dorothy and I were friends in the old neighborhood a long time ago?" It was evident that he was using their old names – Dorothy and Flash – to keep her in the right timeframe.

This was the most talkative that the three had seen Dorothy. Her thoughts were somewhat disjointed but still understandable. Sam kept leading her to talk about the old neighborhood.

"Remember the Paper Rex Man, Dorothy?" he asked and she giggled with the memory. "If I had his horse and cart I could have sold a lot more groceries," she stated. "I just had the stroller and when she grew up some my daughter helped me carry the groceries. She loved that horse."

This was the first that any of them had heard her speak about her daughter. They exchanged glances with the doctor whose expression let them know to be very careful in their approach. Sam slowly asked, "Ah yes, your daughter. What was her name again?"

"Annie. My angel Annie," she replied with a glazed expression. "Of course," the doctor nudged, "everyone called her Anna

Cat, right?" Dorothy frowned. I never cared for that name but her fa…" and she broke off. "A friend gave her that nickname but she will always be Annie to me."

"If I recall," the doctor continued, "she was a beautiful young girl." "Too beautiful!" Dorothy replied with a pained expression and she retreated into silence and rocking back and forth. That was enough for the day and a nurse's aide came to help Dorothy back to her room.

Chapter 32 – The Present

Ren and DJ chattered in the car on the way back teasing each other that they too were "too beautiful." "It's a curse, Deej," Ren guffawed. "But I have learned to live with it." Peggy was uncharacteristically quiet. As the guys banter continued Peggy interrupted them. "Drive to Margaret's office. I have an idea." She said it so forcefully yet calmly that DJ immediately changed lanes and headed toward 32nd and Chester.

"What's the idea?" DJ asked, pulling into the parking lot. The Margaret Wong and Associates LLC building was an impressive structure. It was only one of seven locations for the firm but it was the home office. Margaret Wong was always in demand from groups who wanted to hear her story of turning what was once a single desk rented for $25 into one of the nation's premier immigration law firms.

"Uh, guys," Ren said. "Do you think Margaret is sitting there waiting for us, with not even an appointment, to come in and bother her? She could be in New York or Atlanta or Nashville or even in court."

Despite that, Ren and DJ followed Peggy to the second floor lobby of the building. They saw that she was determined and it was always a treat to visit the building. The lobby was full of beautiful Chinese artifacts and numerous plaques and proclamations that Margaret had earned. There was even a Year of the Pig statue. As Peggy strode toward the reception desk, Ren headed for the bowl of oranges that were on a table and grabbed three. He started peeling one and put the other two in his pockets.

DJ scolded him with his eyes but Ren mouthed, "You can never have too much luck!" Mandarin oranges are a traditional symbol of luck in Chinese culture. The Mandarin pronunciation of the fruit (ju) sounds like the word for "good luck" (ji). The Cantonese pronunciation (gam) is the same as the word "gold." Either way, Ren wasn't taking any chances on missing out on luck.

Peggy asked the receptionist if she could speak to Margaret and, not surprisingly, was politely told that she was unavailable but they could schedule an appointment for a future date or another attorney might be able to help her. Peggy's shoulders shrank and she said she really needed to speak to Margaret and would try another time. She backed away from the desk, bumping into a woman and knocking the file folders she had been carrying to the ground.

"I'm so sorry," Peggy, blushing profusely, confessed, and knelt down to help the woman pick up the folders. She heard the woman say, "Don't worry Peggy. Accidents happen." Surprised that she knew her name Peggy looked at the woman for the first time and saw that it was Cecilia Wong, head of the firm's accounting department and Margaret's sister.

The three had known Cecilia and many of the others in the Wong family for years and she hugged Peggy and then DJ. She looked at Ren who was busy wiping the juice from the orange from his mouth and then hugged him too. "What are you three up to this time?" she asked, ushering them into an empty office off the lobby.

Peggy began explaining the case and Cecilia stopped her. "Margaret told me about this. We both feel bad for the poor man who was convicted. How can we help?"

Peggy explained that they needed some documents from the case and had hoped Margaret could get it for them. They didn't know how to access them or even if they were able to. "Margaret is in court now but let me see what I can do", Cecilia offered. She pulled out her phone and texted something. Within a minute she had received a response – from Margaret. Cecilia sent a few more texts and told the three to sit tight.

"Have an orange while you wait. They are good luck, right Ren?" Ren squirmed in his seat but nodded in the affirmative.

Cecilia left the room laughing and Ren and DJ immediately asked Peggy why she needed all the witness statements. "Henry admits he was the one that got beat up, Peggy" Ren reminded her. Peggy just shrugged and said, "I have an idea. Have another orange." And all three laughed.

In about 15 minutes, Gordon Landefeld, jack-of-many-trades in the office, appeared with a flash drive and a bag. "Margaret had one of her assistants get a copy of the reports," he said and handed the flash drive to Peggy. The three thanked him and asked him to be sure to thank Margaret and Cecilia for the help. As they headed for the door Gordon stopped them and said, "Cecilia wanted you to have this Ren" and handed him the bag. "She said 'Good Luck.'"

They didn't have to be the Mod Squad to decipher the contents of the bag without opening it. It was full of oranges.

Chapter 33 – The Present

Back at the office, they put the flash drive in a computer and opened the pdf files. The document had been drafted by Henry's public defender attorney Jack Johnson. There didn't seem to be anything new. "What are we looking for Peggy? What's your new idea?" DJ asked.

Peggy scrolled down until she saw the witness descriptions. "Here we go" she exhaled. Several witnesses had seen the beating of Henry, which the report had listed as a fight. "How could it be a fight when a bunch of guys jump one person?" Ren asked angrily.

There could be no doubt about the witness accounts of the fight/beating because Henry told the exact same story. But it was the witnesses' reports of the murder scene that Peggy was looking for.

All the witnesses agreed that they saw the Chinese man, Henry, at the scene. They commented on his familiar Chinese jacket with the dragon on it and the black ponytail. His bicycle was there too – with the basket for food deliveries and the dragons painted on the side.

"Peggy," DJ said dejectedly, "We already know all this. The witnesses all checked out and described the same story. Maybe Henry killed him and then blacked out in anger and repressed the memory. "

"No." Ren said. "Henry didn't do it. There has to be another answer."

"And I know what it is," Peggy replied triumphantly.

Ren and DJ stared at Peggy in surprise. "Tell us!" they both demanded. "Ok, Ok," Peggy replied, enjoying the moment. "All the witnesses agree on a few items – Henry's bicycle, his jacket and his description."

"Yes, we know," Ren interrupted. "They saw Henry in his jacket with his bicycle. The physical description fit too – height, build, hair color, ponytail and so on. What am I missing?"

"It's not what you're missing," Peggy answered. "It's what Henry was missing." The two men looked at each other with expressions indicating they felt their friend had lost it.

Exasperated, Peggy scrolled through the document again to Henry's mugshot. "What's missing?" she asked.

There were two mugshots, one from the front and one from the side. They guys stared at the photos and Peggy again asked, "What's missing?"

It took another minute but then they both realized what Peggy had discovered. What was missing was Henry's ponytail. The side view mugshot confirmed what Henry had said about Marko cutting off his ponytail.

"So if the witnesses saw someone with a ponytail at the crime scene it couldn't be Henry because he no longer had his ponytail. Marko had cut it off!" Peggy said triumphantly.

After a round of high-fives they started throwing out ideas. Since Henry had limped home after the beating, both his bike and jacket had been left at Dana's parking lot.

"Somebody could have taken his bike and jacket and the witnesses could have seen another Chinese guy with them by the crime scene," Ren said.

"Or not another Chinese guy or even a guy at all," Peggy corrected. "Just someone who from the back was about Henry's size, wearing his jacket and with his bike. And…" she paused for effect, "with a black ponytail.

Here's what I think happened."

Chapter 34 – The Present

The three called Dr. Norton the next day and asked if they could come talk to him. He agreed and they explained their theory to him and asked his opinion.

"It's certainly possible," he admitted "but how do we get confirmation and proof? We need Dorothy to tell us what happened and I really don't think she is capable of it. The story may be so horrible that she just can't tell it."

"But I can," Peggy replied. And they explained their strategy to the doctor. He was reluctant to have Dorothy go through this but when they stressed how Henry had been imprisoned wrongfully for decades he relented. He told them he would call them as soon as Dorothy was having a "good day."

That came two days later and the three joined the Doctor and Dorothy in a common room. "Hi Flash," they greeted the Doctor. They wanted Dorothy to be thinking in the past as much as possible so they would call him Flash. They had brought some cookies and Peggy casually asked the Doctor – Flash – about growing up in the old neighborhood. She said they were looking to move their office there and had some questions.

The Doctor performed well as he transformed into Flash. He spoke about the schools and churches and some of the stores. He'd look at Dorothy as he spoke for confirmation and she would often nod in agreement. When he mentioned Stanley's Deli her face lit up and she said what a nice, and handsome, man Stanley was.

They didn't want to tire Dorothy out but didn't want to jump to the final act too soon either. After more reminiscing about the old neighborhood around 30th and Payne Peggy asked the Doctor about a story she had heard about some bad men who hung around the school on 26th and Superior and bothered the young girls.

"Yes, unfortunately that's true," the Doctor played along. "It wasn't just the St Columbkille schoolgirls either. There were two brothers who seemed to bother any young girl in the neighborhood." They all noticed that Dorothy stiffened as she heard this. He went on. "Do you remember that Dorothy? Miro and Marko? They were the ones who called me Flash and teased me and poor Peanuts Popcorn Bobbie and so many others." Dorothy just stared blankly and they were afraid they were losing her.

Peggy took a chance and jumped in. "When I was a little girl about twelve years old there were some men in the neighborhood who always looked funny at me and said some rude things. I didn't understand what was going on at the time, I was only twelve, but my mom told me to stay away from them and to be careful. I was always glad that my Mom looked out for me. It was just the two of us you know."

"It's important to have concerned and protective parents, especially mothers, isn't it Dorothy?" the doctor asked. After a pause, Dorothy looked at Peggy and said, "Did they ever do anything to you – you know, bad things?" "No, I was lucky," Peggy answered, "But I know my Mom would have done anything to get them if they had – even kill them."

It seemed that everyone had stopped breathing, waiting for a confession from Dorothy. After what seemed like forever Dorothy nodded and said "I would have killed anyone who hurt my Annie, my Angel Annie. But I didn't have to."

Chapter 35 – The Present

It seemed as if something had broken free in Dorothy's mind and she was remembering the events that she had repressed decades ago. She took a deep breath and said, "Yes, Flash, I remember Miro and Marko. They were just bad, evil men. The way they looked at me and the things they said were shameful. But I was used to it. I had been called every name in the book because I wasn't married when I had Annie but it was different – worse – when it came from them.

I ignored them as much as possible. I was always glad when that handsome fireman was around. Bud was his name. Sweeney I think. Bud Sweeney. I felt safe around him. His friend Seamus was nice too and of course Annie's fa – Stanley from the delicatessen – always helped us out.

So we managed but when Annie grew up a little the catcalls and looks started being directed to her as well as me. I hated that and I hated them for doing it. I tried to cover up Annie as much as possible with loose clothes that we got from the boy's section when the Church had their donation nights. She was growing fast but except for our matching black ponytails she could pass for a boy in those baggy clothes."

Dr. Norton/Flash and the trio were on the edge of their seats, hardly breathing. This was taking an unexpected turn. Could it be?

Dorothy looked at Peggy and took her hand. "I wish I had told my Annie more about being careful around men like that like your mother did," she sobbed. "Why?" Peggy asked gently.

"One night," she went on, "I was at the laundromat and Annie didn't want to go. She wanted to be outside in the fresh air instead of in that stuffy place. I shouldn't have left her alone!"

"When I was done with the laundry I went outside looking for her but she wasn't around. I checked with neighbors and at the stores. I even poked my head into Dana's where I heard about the beating that poor Henry had received. I kept walking, looking for my daughter, my Angel Annie.

I headed toward the railroad tracks fearing the worst and then I saw Henry in the distance. I ran up to him to ask him if he'd seen Annie but… it wasn't Henry. It was my Annie. She was about the same size as the young man and for some reason was wearing his jacket. With her black ponytail in the back she could have been his twin.

Annie was standing over the body of Marko. She had a rock in her hand and a strange, calm expression on her face. 'I killed him Mommy' she said matter of factly.

I didn't know what had happened but I had to get my daughter out of there. I told Annie to take off the jacket and run home as fast as she could and not say anything to anyone.

I remembered hearing about the murders by the train tracks so I took a book of matches from Marko's Pall Mall pack and tried to burn the body. It only caught fire for a few minutes, enough time to scorch a dead rat that was there, but not to burn Marko. I'll never forget that smell.

I looked around for anything that Annie might have left. I took the bloody rock and jacket and started running home. I threw them in a sewer and finally made it home.

'What happened?' I begged Annie. She was calm. Too calm."

Dorothy continued with what Annie had told her. She wanted to go for a walk while Dorothy was doing the laundry. It was cool but nice out. When she got near Dana's she saw Henry's bike leaning against a wall. When she got closer, Marko came out of Dana's and told her that Henry was looking for her. He said that Henry had some food that he wanted to give them. He told her he was over by the tracks and it would be a nice surprise for her mother.

Annie said she agreed and Marko pushed the bike as they walked to the tracks. He gave her Henry's jacket to put on because she was shivering. Maybe he wasn't such a bad guy after all she thought."

"But he was," Dorothy sobbed. "He was the worst. He lured my Angel Annie to the tracks and she said that he started touching her and doing things she knew were wrong. "Annie told me that he wouldn't stop so she picked up a rock and hit him in the head till he stopped."

Chapter 36 – The Present

The five of them sat there in silence. After a moment, Peggy hugged Dorothy and the two of them sobbed in each other's arms. There must have been something in the air because the three men had to turn away and wipe their eyes as well.

Dorothy said that she made Annie promise that she would never speak of what happened that night. "I couldn't let my Annie go to jail for murder, could I? I cry every night about poor Henry and his family but I had to protect my Annie, my Angel Annie.

She was never the same after that night. She never spoke about it but she didn't speak much at all after that. She helped me with the groceries for a few more years, carrying the shopping bags, but never went back to school or made friends. One day she just disappeared.

I looked for her everywhere. Someone told me they thought they saw her up by East Blvd. walking around the Cultural

Gardens but I couldn't find her. I never saw my angel again. My Angel Annie."

Dorothy looked exhausted and Dr. Norton, no longer needing to be called Flash, said that was enough for the day. He summoned a nurse and after hugs all around she was wheeled back to her room.

"I'll check in with her and let her caseworker and doctors know the traumatic experience she just went through," the Doctor said. "Hopefully it's cathartic and she can be at peace. If only they had gone to the authorities. It is clearly a case of self-defense."

"I'm wiped out too," the doctor said "so I will talk to you kids later. I expect that should be enough to free Henry from prison." Ren told him he had turned on his voice recorder on his phone so had it all recorded. The Doctor nodded and shuffled off to his room looking like he had been in a war.

That's how DJ, Ren and Peggy felt too. They were thrilled to know that Henry would be freed but were emotionally drained and felt so bad for the tragic lives of Dorothy and her daughter Annie. Angel Annie. In the car on the way back they were silent for a while and then Peggy asked what they were all thinking. "Could it be? It has to be, right?"

Chapter 37 – The Present

They weren't hungry but realized they needed something to eat so they headed for Pho Row on Superior just east of East 30th. Pho is a Vietnamese soup dish consisting of broth, rice noodles (bánh phở), herbs, and usually beef. It is considered Vietnam's national dish.

They knew that the word "pho" was actually pronounced like "fuh" not "foe" but with 3 similar restaurants on the block it naturally became known to most as the rhyming "Pho Row".

Not to Gia Hoa Ryan and Joe Meissner though. Luong Thi Gia Hoa Ryan was born in Viet Nam, the oldest of twelve children. She worked for the U.S. Government as Interpreter and Secretary during the Vietnam War and supervised local workers for the U.S. Government. She immigrated to United States in 1971.

Gia Hoa was the founder and Executive Director of the Friendship Foundation of American-Vietnamese which has conducted dozen of missions to Vietnam, sponsored over 1,000 volunteer workers, and provided millions in funds, supplies, medicines, medical equipment, services, and other assistance to Vietnam.

She is assisted by attorney and retired Lt. Colonel Joseph Patrick Meissner. Joe was a Green Beret and served in Vietnam. The country and people have remained in his heart and for decades since the war he has used his legal acumen to help the local Vietnamese community as well as those in Vietnam.

As the three entered Superior Pho, one of the Pho Row restaurants, they saw Gia Hoa and Joe at a corner table. There was a steady flow of people approaching their table to pay respects or ask for help.

They said "hi" to the pair who were still very loyal to South Vietnam and Saigon. For example, they would never call Saigon its post-war name Ho Chi Minh City.

With the partition of Vietnam in 1954, over a million people fled North Vietnam for South Vietnam. So phở started to differ by noodle width, sweetness of broth, and choice of herbs and sauce.

The three found a table in another corner and Ren and DJ asked for hot Sriracha sauce and extra jalapenos and lime. Peggy asked for hers with lots of mung bean sprouts and basil.

After placing their order, Ren sent a text to Margaret Wong telling her that they had conclusive proof that Henry was innocent. Within minutes, Margaret responded that they should send her the evidence and she would start the process to exonerate and free Henry.

As they waited for the pho Peggy finally blurted out what she had asked in the car, "Could it be? It has to be, right?" The other two nodded in agreement. "It has to be" agreed DJ.

While working on their project in the Cleveland Cultural Gardens, and solving a series of murders there, the three had come across a homeless woman who frequented, maybe lived, among the flowers, trees and statues of the 35 or so ethnic heritage gardens.

She was a gentle soul but obviously life had not been kind to her. The three befriended her and even helped clear her when she was thought to be a suspect in the murders. Tragically she fell victim to the murderer herself.

The three had often discussed what might have happened to the kind, sad woman in her life to end up like she did. They hoped she was finally at peace. Given what people called her, Peggy liked to think that she was a guardian angel watching over her beloved Cultural Gardens.

Annie. Angel Annie.

Epilogue - The Past

Bud Sweeney never forgot the case of the murders in Chinatown. With his dozens of years of service as a fire fighter and the countless people he had saved over the years he always felt bad that he couldn't help that poor Chinese kid.

Bud and his wife Helen went on to have a terrific life with their growing family. Their daughter Pat married a big strong guy named Norm (but everyone called him Slim) and they had 3 kids of their own. Bud and Helen's son James Francis Jr. became a successful lawyer and married Pam and had 6 kids. Terry followed in his father's footsteps and became a Cleveland firefighter.

Most of the others from the neighborhood had passed on. Ever since her revelation, Dorothy's mental state improved and she and Dr. Norton – she still called him Flash – were able to talk about the good times in the old neighborhood. She could not believe the transformation of the area around 30th and Payne when the Doctor organized a field trip lunch to the area. She had brought 2 roses with her. She placed one near the spot where her daughter Annie had been attacked and another by the site of Stanley's Delicatessen.

Epilogue – Now

It had been a couple of weeks since Henry had been released from the Mansfield Reformatory. Only Margaret Wong could have arranged his release so quickly. The three had let him spend time with his family and get acclimated to the outside world before contacting him again. Ren had promised Henry a tour of Cleveland's new AsiaTown and they had driven him around several times.

Since his release, Henry had been depressed about all the things and people he had missed over the years but he was very grateful to the three young people for their efforts to free him – and, more importantly, to clear his family name.

On their latest tour, Peggy spoke non-stop as they drove up I-77 but the guys didn't tease her – Henry was very interested.

As they neared Cleveland, Henry's eyes lit up. He remembered the Terminal Tower and marveled at it again as they approached. Terminal Tower is a 52-story, 708 ft. skyscraper right on Public Square in the center of downtown Cleveland. When it was completed in 1927 it was the second-tallest building in the world. Terminal Tower remained as the tallest building in North America outside of New York City from its completion in 1927 until 1964. On a clear day, visitors on the observation deck can see 30 miles away.

Henry had seen it when movies were shown in the prison such as The Deer Hunter, A Christmas Story, Major League and others as well as The Avengers and Spider-Man-3 which were partly filmed in Cleveland. He also saw it in TV reruns of The Drew Carey Show and Hot in Cleveland but he had yearned to see it again in person.

What he could not imagine was that, at least from the distance of the freeway, it did not dominate the Cleveland skyline anymore. Peggy was happy to point out that in 1991 a new skyscraper, Key Tower, was completed.

Originally known as Society Center, Key Tower reaches 57 stories or 947 feet to the top of its spire. Ren checked Wikipedia on his phone and added, "It is the tallest building in the state of Ohio, the 39th-tallest in the United States, and the 165th-tallest in the world." Terminal Tower was still the second-tallest building in the state but it was noticeably shorter than Key Tower in the skyline.

Peggy explained that hundreds of LED lights on the Terminal Tower could be configured into various color schemes, such as red and green during the Christmas season and red, white and blue for various federal holidays. Some of Cleveland's ethnic groups have had the Terminal Tower lit in their traditional colors, such as green on Saint Patrick's Day. On Polish Constitution Day the tower is white and red (Polish flag colors), and the tower goes red, green, and white (Italian flag colors) for Columbus Day.

DJ added that when the Browns, Cavaliers or Guardians played it would showcase their colors. Henry was awestruck. He sat in silence and then asked, "What are the Guardians?" The three laughed and explained the Cleveland baseball team's name change from Indians to Guardians.

As they got off the freeway, the trio drove around downtown pointing out landmarks and additions such as the Rock and Roll Hall of Fame. But Henry was eager to see Chinatown.

He was visibly disappointed as they pulled onto Rockwell at East 21st. There were still some restaurants and stores and there were stone statues of the Chinese Zodiac animals but he had expected more after all these years.

"Don't worry," Ren said. "Wait till you see AsiaTown!" They drove up Superior and as they approached East 26th Henry blurted, "Where is St. Columbkille's?" They explained that St. Columbkille's Church and School were razed in 1957 for construction of the Inner Belt Freeway (Interstate 90). Henry just shook his head but his eyes lit up as they approached East 30th and Payne.

This, of course, had been the corner where Dana's Bar had been. Now it was Asia Plaza with restaurants, community resources and beautiful murals and was attached to a huge Asian/Chinese grocery store.

On one trip they took Henry for dim sum at Li Wah but today they just grabbed a treat from Ball Ball Waffle in the center of Asia Plaza to tide them over. These bubble waffles were popular street foods in Hong Kong and now were a favorite in Cleveland.

They had already told Henry about the Cleveland Asian Festival founded by Johnny Wu, Lisa Wong and Vi Huyn, which annually attracts 50,000 visitors to Asia Plaza but this was the first time he could visualize how that was possible on the former site of that old bar.

They drove up to see the Chinese Cultural Garden with the large statue of Confucius and were fortunate to catch the tail end of another performance by the Kwan Family Lion Dance Team there. They grabbed some steamed buns from a food truck while they watched. Ren made sure to feed the Lion with a red envelope with a few dollars for luck.

It had been a whirlwind few visits. Lots of Chinese food and cultural stops. DJ and Peggy caught Ren staring at Henry several times on their visits. They figured he was wondering if he was going to look like that in the future. After all, their uncanny resemblance had been what started this whole adventure.

They were tired and knew that these outings wouldn't make up for the many years that Henry was in prison but they wanted to do all they could to make it up to him.

Back in the car, DJ leaned over and asked, "What else do you want to see, Henry?"

Henry said "You don't know how much I thank you kids for all you have done for me and my family name. And these visits to Chinatown – and AsiaTown - have been overwhelming. I can't believe how things have changed. But to tell you the truth, I've had so much Chinese food lately that I could really go for a pizza!"

DJ, Ren and Peggy laughed and DJ made a quick turn. "We're off to Little Italy!" he shouted. None of the three could know that that was the site of their next adventure.

The End.

Author's note

Much of the descriptions of places and buildings are accurate but some literary license had been employed. The murder is fictional but the history of Chinatown, AsiaTown, Asia Plaza and so on is based on facts. Cleveland's AsiaTown and the Cleveland Asian Festival are not only real but a must-visit location and event.

Some of the characters such as Margaret Wong, and the author's grandfather James "Bud" Sweeney and his family are based on real people but again, this is a work of fiction and it is not intended to be a verbatim account.

The Sweeney's did live on East 32nd between Payne and Perkins and attended St. Columbkille's Church. The descriptions of the neighborhood and fireman Bud Sweeney are also based on fact. Bud's son-in-law Norm (aka Slim, married to his daughter Pat) established his electrical business at East 32nd and Payne and ran it for decades. The author also started his businesses at that location and worked there for years.

If you missed the first book with DJ, Ren and Peggy - Murder in the Cultural Gardens – you can find it on Amazon, local bookstores or write the author at 868 Montford Rd. Cleveland Heights OH 44121. That and future adventures of DJ, Ren and Peggy can be found at www.danhansonbooks.com.

Made in the USA
Columbia, SC
12 November 2024

46177225R00085